SPRING'S SECOND CHANCE ✿

by

J. Sterling

Angela,
this book is my
favorite of the bunch!
Hope you like it

xox J. St.

SPRING'S SECOND CHANCE

Copyright © 2022 by J. Sterling

Edited by:

Jovana Shirley

Unforeseen Editing

www.unforeseenediting.com

Cover Design by:

Michelle Preast

www.Michelle-Preast.com

www.facebook.com/IndieBookCovers

Other Books by J. Sterling

WEDDING COUNTDOWN

SPRING

I FIDDLED WITH the diamond engagement ring on my left hand, twisting it and turning it until my sister, Dee—short for Delilah—yelled at me to stop. I'd been doing it a lot lately, and if I'd thought she wasn't paying attention, clearly, I was mistaken.

"What is wrong with you?" she asked. Her long auburn hair, which matched the color of my own, swished back and forth in her ponytail as she stopped filling a cupcake pan to stare at me.

Dee always wore a ponytail high on top of her head, insisting that it never gave her a headache, but every time I tried to copy her, I got tension aches within the hour. And even though we looked so much alike that people often mistook us for twins, she looked sexy and sassy with her hair that way, whereas I looked childish. Like a preteen cheerleader trying desperately to look cute.

"Nothing. Why? What's wrong with you?" I snapped back, tugging at my two braids, pretending to be reading a recipe that I already knew by heart.

She propped her hip against the counter before scouting the few tables and chairs inside the bakery walls. It was currently empty, and she gave me an almost-wistful look. "Your wedding is in five weeks," she said, as if I didn't have a countdown going on my phone, on every calendar, or in my splintering heart.

"I know that," I said, twisting the simple diamond ring again.

This had nothing to do with the ring and everything to do with the guy who had given it to me.

Or maybe it had nothing to do with him at all and everything to do with the girl wearing the ring.

Dee and I had grown up in Lake Bliss, a tiny mountain town in the hills of California. Whenever most people thought about California, they usually imagined Los Angeles, San Diego, or San Francisco. But over the last five years, Lake Bliss had changed from a small tourist town, only visited by regulars each year, into one of the most coveted places to vacation and buy property, if you were lucky enough to come across someone selling, which used to not happen often.

Lake Bliss had always been a diverse community, where families who'd originally moved there ended up never leaving. Their kids stayed and raised their families and so on and so forth. Houses and land were passed down from generation to generation, rarely falling into the hands of a stranger unless there was no family left. And even then, the property was usually snatched up by a local. This didn't happen from a standpoint of greed, but more of an old-school preservation state of mind. *Blissens*, as the elder townspeople affectionately called themselves, didn't want to see Lake Bliss change. And they fought hard to keep it the way it had always been—idyllic, and basically hidden in plain sight.

That all changed after an article in a magazine, talking about "California's Best-Kept Secrets," named Lake Bliss as its number one hidden gem a handful of years back. That publication turned our little town on its head. We were overrun the first year after the piece came out, completely unable to handle the number of tourists who had suddenly flocked here overnight, wanting to stay the weekend and purchase vacation homes. There weren't enough motels for them to stay in. Not enough restaurants for them to eat at. What had been serving our community perfectly for the last hundred or so years had come to a screeching halt.

If any of us Blissens had thought that the surge would die down after a couple of seasons, we were dead wrong. The magazine had given way to numerous blog posts and online travel articles. Lake Bliss was suddenly on the map with no plans of leaving it.

Our town had quickly doubled in size after a handful of the townspeople sold their land to big resorts and condo developers—our parents being one of them. They only sold off half of the family land, but it was enough to upset some of the other locals that they'd sell anything to strangers at all. Others understood. Those businessmen paid life-changing money to the families who had said yes.

Our parents had hightailed it out of California and relocated to Arizona at first before finally settling somewhere near the ocean in Florida. They claimed to love the humidity and the low cost of living. All we knew was that they were happy and seemed to be living their best lives. They texted us pictures almost every day, smiling, laughing, drinks in hand. They'd even bought a boat. Dad caught them dinner five nights a week.

Selling had been a good thing for them. It gave them a

new lease on life with the freedom to explore, travel, and do whatever they wanted. That was probably why I found the idea of change coming to Lake Bliss more than a little inviting. And I knew I wasn't the only one.

The younger generations of Blissens liked having all the new blood in town. It shook up our pond, as someone had once said. I wasn't supposed to like any of the new guys who flitted in and out, flirting with me and my sister at our bakery, but even I had to admit that it was exciting.

Up until that point, everyone in Lake Bliss had known everyone else. We'd all grown up together since birth practically. Which was why Dee claimed to never have a boyfriend after middle school.

"They're like family at this point. I just don't see any of them in that way," she'd told me one time.

And for the most part, I agreed.

Until the summer after ninth grade, when Mitchell Flores had somehow turned from a boy into a guy overnight. Mitchell had spent the summer working for his dad's construction company, and it had done him good. He came back to school five inches taller, even more tanned than his naturally golden skin allowed, and full of defined muscles, where there'd been nothing more than skinny sticks before. I thought I'd drooled at the sight of him on that first day back.

He wasn't the only one who had changed that summer. I finally got actual boobs … as opposed to the tiny molehills I'd previously sported. Dee had sprouted her C-cups in, like, seventh grade, so waiting years for mine to catch up had been torture. But once they were there, I understood what she'd been telling me the whole time as I lamented to her, doing *I must, I must, I must increase my bust* exercises every night.

"Boobs are annoying, Spring. And boys forget you have eyes," she'd warned, but I never understood what the heck she was talking about.

Until I got them myself.

Boys stopped looking at my face while they talked to me, their eyes solely focused on my chest and what was hidden beneath my shirt. Everyone—except Mitchell, that was. He seemed to remember that I had eyes because he oscillated between looking me in mine and at my boobs when we spoke.

He'd asked me out, and one date was all it had taken. We were inseparable after that.

And now, here I was, falling into some age-old tradition that everyone said was the right thing to do. What other choice did I have? You dated, got engaged, got married, bought a house, had babies, and then you died.

"Spring? Hello? Earth to Spring." Dee's voice pulled me from my thoughts.

"I'm here," I said, shaking my head.

I knew there was no use in lying to her. My sister saw through my words, especially when they weren't true.

"But you're not. What's going on with you? You know you can tell me anything." She placed a hand on my shoulder, and I hadn't even realized she'd stepped closer until she took the bag of frosting from my grip.

I looked down and realized that I'd used almost the entire piping bag on one cupcake. "Dammit," I said, pulling my hand away.

"You're distracted. Are you pregnant?" she asked, and I started slapping at my chest like I might choke.

"God, no. Don't say that," I yelled, sounding angry even though I wasn't.

"Then. What. Is. It?" she pushed. Dee was good at pushing. Which was half the reason why our bakery had been so successful in the first place.

Dee was an absolute goddess when it came to building our brand. She handled every bit of the marketing and met with our local vendors, some farms not too far away, and eventually event planners in every arena of business to make sure that our bakery was the go-to stop for all things weddings, birthdays, anniversaries, et cetera. Not like there were many options, considering the fact that the two other bakeries in town only made breads and pastries, but still, Dee left them no choice. It was either us or the grocery store, and no one in their right mind was going to have stale cupcakes when they could have fresh, one-of-a-kind creations by yours truly. Dee said that I was a *culinary genius of baking*.

We had opened our store, Bliss Bakery, about a year before the tourist boom, both of us taking online business classes while I was still wrapping up my senior year of high school. The idea for the store had come to life after I wanted fancy cupcakes for my birthday party in a tier, like I'd kept seeing online. But no one in our town made those, so Dee said we'd grow up and make them ourselves.

And we did.

We had been popular since the day our doors had first opened, the townspeople all too willing to support two of their own starting a new business venture. The town's diversity was such a blessing, teaching me about various cultures and authentic flavors and spices. I had met with the elders of the community, taking my time in getting to know their traditions so that I could incorporate their spices into my cakes, if possible. Bliss Bakery was unlike anyplace else with flavor combinations that honored a multitude of traditions.

"We only have a dozen more, and then the Pavlo anniversary party is done." She smiled, trying to make me feel better even though I felt like I was unraveling inside.

It kept getting worse—this feeling. I'd been good at hiding it the last few weeks, but the past few days had become almost unbearable.

And there was no good reason for it either. Mitchell Flores was a good man, poised to take over and run his father's construction company one day. Flores Construction received most of the winning bids within Lake Bliss. They were making a killing with the boom and earning the kind of money that, by any standards, would be considered wealthy.

Mitchell worked hard, was handsome, and I trusted him implicitly. Even when other girls had hit on him over the years, he never strayed, and as far as I knew, he was never even tempted. Like I'd said, he was a good man. The kind of guy that any girl would be lucky to call her own. He would make a fantastic husband and a great father someday.

But every time I so much as thought those words lately, my stomach revolted, threatening to bowl me over in excruciating pain. Something was wrong. Something I didn't want to admit because there was no good reason for it. I felt like even having these thoughts made me a bad person somehow.

Maybe it's just cold feet, I thought to myself for the hundredth time, but the visceral reaction that twisted in my guts let me know that it wasn't that at all. It wasn't cold feet. I wasn't scared. I just simply … didn't want this anymore.

I was only twenty-four years old. Mitchell and I had been together since I was fifteen. That made nine years. Nine years with the same person … with the only person. Instead of feeling secure and happy, it made me feel trapped and suffocated. Like I had nothing to look forward to anymore. Everything seemed so set in stone, so mapped out, so unable to be changed.

"I don't want to marry Mitchell," I blurted out so quickly that I even surprised myself by saying it. I couldn't take it back now. The words were in the air, hanging between my sister and me.

"I know," was all she said before the bell jingled on the door, and I looked up to see my handsome fiancé walking through it, a giant smile on his face.

BREAKING HEARTS

SPRING

"THERE'S MY BEAUTIFUL bride-to-be," Mitchell said before walking straight past the employee counter and into the back, where I stood, forcing a smile.

He reached for me, his hands gripping my waist as he pulled me up into the air and planted a hard kiss on my lips, just like he always did.

This man loved me. Truly loved me.

And I'd just admitted to my sister, no less than ten seconds prior, that I didn't want to marry him.

What kind of monster am I?

I searched for Dee's face, her eyes widening as she silently pleaded for me to do ... *something*. I had no idea what though. I couldn't interpret her expression.

"You girls almost done for the night?" Mitchell asked before stepping back on the proper side of the counter.

"We just have a dozen more," Dee said for me since I seemed to have lost my voice somewhere between my admittance of not wanting a fiancé any longer and said fiancé kissing the information out of me. "But I can handle that if you want to go," she urged, and I finally understood what she was trying to tell me.

Talk to him, her expression pleaded.

Tell him, it pushed even more.

Call it off, it begged.

They were all things that had been consuming my mind day in and day out recently, but saying the actual words out loud, to him, seemed impossible. I knew that once they passed my lips and crashed into his ears, I'd never be able to take them back. And what if I was wrong or making a mistake?

Mitchell would be devastated. Especially when I had no reason to not want to go through with the wedding other than …

It doesn't feel right anymore.

There would be a hundred questions that I wouldn't have answers for. So many things that he'd want to know, like where it'd all gone wrong or when my feelings had changed, and I wouldn't be able to pinpoint a single moment to explain why my heart suddenly wanted out of something it had loved being in for so long.

He'd want concrete evidence, proof, and facts to be able to make sense of what I was telling him, but there would be none. I wouldn't have any of those things to offer him, except my feelings, emotions, and gut instincts that screamed so loud that they refused to be ignored any longer. But how did you make someone accept reason when what I was saying was so *un*reasonable?

"Do you want to stay, Spring? Or do you want to head to my place? Or grab some dinner?" Mitchell asked, his eyes letting me know that he'd be fine with whichever option I chose.

My only saving grace in all of this was that I hadn't moved in with him. I kept putting that off until we were actually married, telling him that we needed at least one thing to stay sacred and that cohabitating was my solution. He begrudgingly agreed but only because he'd started building us our dream house. From scratch. With his own two hands. We were supposed to move in and start our life together in less than two months.

The bile rose in my throat, and I looked at my sister once more, her hazel eyes giving me strength.

"Go." She waved us off. "It's only one dozen. I can handle that."

"I know you can," I said with an awkward smile. "But the store still has an hour before closing."

"It's fine. The tourists aren't here yet," she pushed, knowing that I'd have no ground to argue.

The tourists came twice a year—winter and summer. We had gorgeous, fluffy snowflakes that served as the perfect backdrop for winter weddings, and during the summer, our lake was the centerpiece of the whole town, showing off her various shades of blue.

"See you later, Dee." Mitchell waved at my sister, his smile taking up his whole face.

"Night, you guys," she said before clamping her mouth shut tight.

If I didn't spend the night at Mitchell's, I'd see her when I got home, and we could talk then.

He reached for my hand, interlaced our fingers, and opened the bakery door for me. "Dinner or my place?" he asked.

I sucked in a breath, hoping it would give me the strength I needed. But my breath failed me. My heart was beating so fast that I thought it might come out of my chest. My head spun. I knew I needed to talk to him about this, to stop it before it was too late, but that was just so damn hard to do. Those particular words were stuck in my throat.

I spotted his truck right out front. "Let's just go to your place," I said, and he looked so happy.

He deserved so much better.

"You okay, Spring?" he asked, his brow furrowed as he opened the door for me and I hopped inside.

My stomach twisted again. I bent my body in half, my hand wrapped around my middle as I squeezed it tight. I might very well throw up on his floor mat.

"Spring?" he said as the driver's door slammed closed. "Are you okay?"

I straightened my body and looked at him. "I …" My eyes watered so hard and fast, and before I knew it, I was crying so hard that I thought I might hyperventilate.

"You what? What's the matter?" His voice sounded so genuinely pained for me as he lovingly rubbed his hand on my back, trying to calm me down.

I tried to wipe away the tears, but there were too many. I stared at the diamond on my hand. I had loved that ring so much at first. When he'd been on one knee, looking up at me through his unfairly long lashes, asking me to marry him, I'd felt so excited and hopeful.

Where were any of those emotions now?

Now, I longed to see my finger bare, with nothing on it. No billboard announcing to the world that I was taken, off the market … unavailable. No ball and chain across my ring finger, dragging me down into the depths of the sea until I drowned in it.

"Spring?"

I moved my eyes from my ring to Mitchell's face. "I don't think I want to get married," I whispered the words so quietly that I secretly hoped he hadn't heard them.

Mitchell reared back in his seat like I'd socked him with a two-by-four. He grabbed the baseball hat from his head and started pulling at it with his hands, twisting like it was a wet rag. "What? You don't want to get married?"

I wasn't sure that I had the determination or strength to say the words again, so I didn't say anything. He swallowed hard, his Adam's apple bobbing in his throat. A throat I had memorized. Could probably draw with my eyes closed if someone asked me to.

"It's just cold feet, babe. That's all. This is totally normal." He almost sounded convinced.

"It's not cold feet," I said, my voice still barely above a whisper.

"Then, what is it?" he asked, his voice breaking, and I swore my heart broke too.

I shook my head. "I don't know. I don't know why. I just know that I don't want to."

A single tear rolled down his cheek, and I hated myself for hurting him. But I knew that I'd have hated myself even more if I'd stayed with him and pretended like this was what I still wanted when it wasn't. Eventually, we'd have found ourselves right back in this place ... me wanting out ... him begging me to stay.

"Did something happen? Did you meet someone?" His voice wasn't angry. It wasn't even remotely mad. It was longing to understand, desperately trying to comprehend how the girl who had been his whole world for nine years suddenly wanted out of it.

"Nothing happened." I reached for his hand and squeezed it hard. "I don't know why I'm feeling like this, but I am."

"Sleep on it," he said.

I knew he was hoping that I'd change my mind tomorrow. That, somehow, another night's sleep would change everything. That I'd wake up, refreshed, heart back in place, walking the proverbial line.

The sweet gesture made me snap though. Here I was, trying to do the hardest thing I'd ever done in my life, and Mitchell was asking me to put it off for another day. He was basically going to force me to tell him all of this again tomorrow. To break his heart another time.

"I've been sleeping on it, Mitchell," I said. "I've been sleeping on it," I repeated the sentiment, feeling exhausted and brokenhearted.

"I don't understand," he said, running his fingers across the top of his head. "I still want this. I still want you. I love you, Spring."

I knew all of those things. God, how I knew all of those things. And I wished that they were enough.

"It doesn't make any sense. I know that. But it's killing me inside, Mitch. I feel like I'm dying," I said, not even stopping to think about how my words might make him feel. They were hurtful even though they were true. He didn't deserve to hear them.

His jaw snapped shut before his eyes narrowed a little. "I'm sorry the idea of marrying me is so revolting to you."

"That's not what I meant," I tried to explain, but it was too late. I'd said too much. I'd pushed too far.

"Just go," he said.

Even though it was exactly what I'd wanted, I felt like the lowest human being on the planet as I pushed out of his truck and watched as he sped away, gravel spitting off of his tires as he left.

NOW WHAT?

SPRING

I STOOD THERE on the sidewalk for a minute, maybe longer, until someone came up behind me and told me how much she was looking forward to the wedding. My wedding. The one I'd just called off.

Forcing a smile, I told her, "Thank you," and quickly spun around on my heels and headed back inside the bakery.

Dee looked up, her eyes widening when she realized it was me. "Oh," she said. "You told him?"

"I told him."

She walked from the back and straight to our front door and locked it before switching the sign to *Closed* and putting the key in her apron pocket. We shouldn't have closed already, but there was no point in arguing with Dee.

"You are the toughest person I know," she said, and it made me wince.

I didn't feel tough. Hurting someone who had done nothing to deserve it didn't make me feel strong. It made me feel cruel.

"Spring, look at me," Dee demanded, and I did as she'd asked. "You did something that took an insane amount of strength. Do you hear me?"

I nodded as she continued, "Most people would have shoved those feelings down and gone through with it anyway, knowing it was wrong or that they didn't want to do it anymore."

"But I don't have a reason, you know? I don't know why I feel this way. I just do," I said, the admittance only making myself feel worse. Everything would have been so much easier to handle emotionally if there had at least been a reason why.

"I know you feel like a bad person right now, but you're not. You did the right thing. If you hadn't done it now, you would have done it eventually. And when? After you had kids and felt even more trapped?"

I listened to her words before remembering that she'd told me she knew I didn't want to marry him. When I had confessed that to her earlier, she had simply said, "I know."

"How did you know?"

"That you wanted out?"

"Yeah. I never said anything."

"You didn't have to. I had a feeling. I mean, you started acting like everything was such a chore," she said, and I swore that I gasped.

"I did?"

"I'm actually not sure if *chore* is the right word. But it was like you did stuff because you were supposed to do it. Not because you wanted to. You seemed …" She tapped her chin, searching for a word. "Obligated? I don't know, but you stopped smiling a while ago, and that smile never came back."

I hadn't realized any of those things. I'd been so caught up in wishing that I could turn my heart around and go back in time. It seemed so much easier that way. This decision was definitely harder.

"I love Mitchell as a person," I started to say, but Dee interrupted me.

"But you're not in love with him," she finished for me.

"Yeah. And that's so cliché that I hate even saying it, but it's the truth. And I never even understood what it meant until now. It always sounded so stupid. But there's a difference. Between loving someone and being in love with them."

"Of course there is. But I think the longer you're with a person, the harder it is to tell those feelings apart," she offered and I bristled, assuming that she thought that I was doing the wrong thing.

"You think I don't know anymore because it's been nine years?"

"No, I'm not saying that at all. I just think for a lot of people, the lines of love become blurred between passion and friendship, but you always know, deep in your bones, that you're still in love with that person. That's not ever a question." I must have made some sort of face in response because she smirked at me and pointed. "See? You're not."

"I'm not. And I know that I'm not with every fiber of my being," I admitted, still feeling crappy.

"Then, you did the right thing." She stepped toward me and placed her hands on my shoulders. "You did the right thing. Mitchell is hurting now, but he'll eventually get over it. You did both of you a favor."

Was that what I'd done? Would Mitchell really ever see it that way, or would he hate me for the rest of his life and never forgive me?

"I should give him back the ring, right?" I looked down at it before pulling it off, feeling my finger grow lighter.

"I would."

"How do I cancel a whole entire wedding?" I asked, feeling the weight land squarely on my shoulders for the first time. It was heavy. Everything had been meticulously planned and paid for.

"I can do all of that for you. Whatever you want. I'll talk to Mom and Dad. Whatever you need, just let me know."

It was official. I had the best older sister in the history of the world.

"The entire town is going to hate me," I said.

Because how did you not pick sides when something like this happened? You did, and they would, and it wasn't going to be mine.

"I can think of ten girls off the top of my head who are going to be thanking you instead of hating you," she said, and I managed to laugh.

"You're not wrong there," I agreed before thinking of all the people I was letting down by making this decision.

Mitchell. His family. Our family. Our friends. The town who had watched us grow up together.

I hadn't thought about any of that before. I'd only been thinking about myself and how I didn't want to walk down the aisle anymore.

"Do you feel relieved?" Dee asked, and I inhaled a sharp

breath.

"I feel ..." I paused. "I don't feel relieved because there's still so much to do. But I feel like I can breathe again, if that makes any sense."

We cleaned the kitchen, wiped down all the tables, and worked in relative silence for the next hour, the two of us taking our time instead of rushing the way we usually did. I was grateful for the reprieve until my phone pinged out a sound, and I looked down, noticing a text from Mitchell.

I glanced up at my sister, who shot me a questioning look.

"Mitchell," I said, turning it around so she could see it was from him before I pressed on the message to read it. "He wants to come over and talk."

"That's a good idea," Dee said. "Do you want me to be there? I'll stay in my room."

"Yeah." I nodded.

"Okay then. Text him that you'll meet him at our place," she said.

We made sure all the ovens were off, the fridge and freezer doors were shut tight, and everything was in place for the night before we headed out the back and locked up.

IT DIDN'T TAKE Mitchell long to arrive at our house. We'd just barely walked through the front door and thrown our purses on the kitchen counter when I heard his truck pull in.

Dee told me, "Good luck," and then she disappeared behind her bedroom door.

Pulling the engagement ring from my pocket, I gently placed it on top of the kitchen table, so I wouldn't forget to give it back to him.

But when Mitchell walked through the door, his eyes landing on the ring and holding there, I thought I might have done the wrong thing. Maybe he still wanted me to take it back or change my mind. The ring sitting there, no longer on my finger, was like a neon sign telling him it was really over.

He pulled out a chair and sat down before reaching for the ring and holding it between two of his fingers. It looked so dainty in his hand. "You can keep it." He put it back down and slid it toward me.

"I don't think that's right. You should have it back," I said, not moving to touch it.

I didn't want the ring, and it didn't belong to me. He'd paid for it. He should be able to take it back and get some money for it.

"Look, Spring, I'm not going to pretend to know what's

going on with you, but if you need more time," he started, and my head shook of its own accord.

"It's not that. I don't need more time. My mind isn't going to change."

He sucked in a breath. "I know. I don't even know why I said that."

"I wish I had a reason, Mitchell. Something that would make this make any kind of sense," I started to explain, but he put his hand up to stop me.

"It's okay."

"It's … *okay*?" I asked, perplexed as to what he might possibly be saying.

"There's a part of me that knows you're doing the right thing," he admitted, looking like it pained him to say it though.

"There is?"

His eyes shot up, meeting mine. "I still love you. And I'd marry you tomorrow. But what if it's because it's all we've ever known? What if we're both just going through the motions?"

My heart skipped a beat as I tried to figure out his exact meaning while he continued, "You're comfortable. I'm comfortable. We're familiar. But is that love? The kind of love that lasts? I don't know. I don't have the answers, but you calling off the wedding"—he swallowed hard, like saying this out loud caused him pain—"I know in my gut that it's the right thing to do. But still …"

I thought he was going to say more, but he stopped.

"Are you just saying this to make me feel better?" I asked through a short laugh because he was truly giving me a gift right now.

"No, Spring." His head shook slowly. "I spent the last hour trying not to be pissed, sorting through my hurt pride and ego."

I leaned forward, both elbows on the table. "I never meant to hurt you."

"I know that," he said, and it made me feel only the tiniest bit better. "I'm not mad that you want to call off the wedding."

"You're not?" I had no idea what the hell was happening, but I knew it was leaning toward being a good thing. One that meant we wouldn't end our relationship on bad terms, where I was hated and despised for the rest of eternity.

"No. I mean, I thought I was. I was really pissed, but then I realized that I felt something else too. I was excited. Excited at the idea of being single for the first time in my adult life. And if you and I getting married were right, I wouldn't be feeling excited at all. You're all I've ever known," he said, stuttering a little, and I knew that meant that he was going to apologize and overexplain his feelings to me, but I didn't need any of that.

"It's okay. You don't have to say anything. I'm not offended. I get it," I said, and he visibly relaxed.

"Is that how you feel? Amped up to date?"

I couldn't tell if he was either curious or simply wanted to be understood. Maybe if we were both on the same page, then it would make this easier to comprehend and move on from.

"Not really. I mean, it's not about being with someone else or meeting someone new for me. I just realized that this"—I waved my finger between our two bodies—"didn't feel right anymore. That taking that next step was going to be a mistake." I clenched my teeth together as I said the last word, but it didn't trigger him like I'd thought it might.

"It's weird, you know? We've been together for so long that it feels like I'm losing an arm or something."

I smiled. "I know. It's like learning life all over again. I grew up with you. Who even am I without you?"

"You're Spring Monroe. Super-successful baker extraordinaire. And you never needed me," he said, and I knew that he was happy for all that I'd built and accomplished. Even now, while we were ending things, he was still proud of me. "Do you think we could tell people that we mutually called it off?" he suggested, and I almost leaped for joy on top of the table.

Did he have any idea how much that would help my state of mind and ease my guilt?

"If that's what you want."

"I think it would be best. And easiest for us both. People won't be mean to you that way. And I'll feel less embarrassed." He winced.

"Thank you," I said, reaching for his hand on the table and squeezing it. "How pissed are our parents going to be?"

He shrugged. "They'll be fine. You know why?"

"Why?"

"Because we are." He pushed back from the chair and stood up.

"The ring," I said. "Take it. Please."

He looked between it and me, like I was asking him to hide a body or something equally as difficult. "Fine. But on one condition."

I had no idea what condition he might suggest, but I gave him a look and asked, "What condition?"

"You take the honeymoon trip," he said, and when I looked confused, he added, "You still go on it."

I hadn't even thought about the damn honeymoon. The one thing that I'd really been looking forward to. That I'd researched and planned and picked specifically to combine both of our wants and desires—but to be honest, mostly mine. I'd wanted to go on that trip so badly, and he knew it. If Mitchell had wanted to hurt me, he would have taken it or given it away.

"Really? You want me to go?"

"I know how much you've wanted to go to Hawaii. It's all I've heard about since the tenth grade. So, yes. Go. You'll probably need a break from Bliss by then anyway," he said before grabbing the ring and hovering it above his pocket. "Deal?"

"Deal," I said, and he slipped it inside.

We stepped toward one another and hugged. It wasn't a *see you later* hug. It wasn't an *until next time*. It was good-bye, and we both knew it. And that relief I'd been hoping to finally feel … well, it enveloped me like a warm blanket, and I finally felt free.

HAWAII, HERE I COME

SPRING

CALLING OFF THE wedding location and vendors had been the easy part. Nothing a few emails and returned checks couldn't handle. But making sure that everyone knew we were no longer getting married was the bitch of it all. No one simply canceled their travel plans, said okay, and carried on with their lives. *No.* Everyone wanted to know why, what had happened, and asked a million and one questions that I couldn't answer—and wouldn't have even if I could. It really wasn't anyone's business.

But telling them that Mitchell and I had realized that we were better off as friends instead of husband and wife wasn't a good enough answer. People refused to accept it, hoping for a reason far more scandalous and decadent to chew on.

But there wasn't one.

And all of the non-drama was too far-fetched for everyone to believe. How could we simply call it off like it was no big deal and smile through it all? Both of us had carried on so easily; it was almost unreal.

My parents had offered to still come out, concerned that I needed them or might have some kind of breakdown, but one phone call was all it had taken to convince them otherwise. I thought they were grateful they didn't have to come back and face everyone who was still mad at them for leaving.

When the day of my actual wedding arrived, I was shocked to find myself nervous. I woke up in chills as sweat dripped down my stomach. It was weird to not be getting married when it was something that I'd been planning and looking forward to for so long. It wasn't that I regretted my decision to call it off; it was just a little emotional, was all.

Dee had tried to tell me to take the day off, to stay home, but the last thing I wanted to do was wallow. She offered to book me a spa day, but I told her that people were still too inquisitive, and I didn't want to spend the whole day feeling judged. I'd ensured her that if it got too painful or hard, being at work, that I'd go home. But to be honest, the bakery had always been my reprieve. I could lose myself in the back, creating new flavors and frosting combinations. I was happiest when I was creating.

So, I went to the bakery with a smile and started going through all of our upcoming orders and mixing various frostings so that Dee wouldn't have to. As long as I put them in airtight containers, they would keep for a week. It was a lot of work for one person, so I tried to help as much as I could before I left.

"I can't believe you get to go to Hawaii for ten days," she said from the front of the bakery, her voice taking on a dreamlike quality.

There had been two tickets, obviously, and I was tempted to invite Dee along, but then we'd have to close the bakery while we were both gone, and we had way too many orders in the queue to do that. Our Mom could have flown and filled in, but neither one of us had wanted to ask.

Plus, Dee had insisted that I take this trip by myself. She said that it would be good for me to be alone with my feelings and work through whatever emotions happened to come up while I was there. I was grateful because a part of me wanted to be by myself with no one to report to or run things by. Living the Hawaiian life on my own timeline, doing whatever I wanted, whenever I wanted it.

"I'll be a pro on all things Hawaii by the time I come back. I'll be able to plan us an even better trip for next time," I suggested, and Dee's face lit up as she nodded.

"Sounds good."

"You sure you don't want to hire extra help while I'm gone?" I asked for the fiftieth time.

"I'm good. If we had any more orders, I might have brought in the big guns, but I can handle all of these. Just promise me you'll go, relax, and have a good time. Enjoy being away from Bliss."

That was one thing I was actually excited about. As much as I loved this town, I rarely left it, and I needed a break from all the prying eyes and gossiping lips that inundated my every day.

Speaking of gossip, I'd heard that Mitchell was already dating. Dee had heard that he'd been on three dates with three different girls since we'd split up. I'd wondered how him moving on was going to make me feel, mostly because he'd been mine for so long, but I was happily surprised when I realized that I just wanted him to be okay. It made me feel settled to know that he was.

It meant that I could be okay too.

THE HONOLULU INTERNATIONAL Airport was hot and humid, the air hitting me before I was prepared for it. Stepping into baggage claim, I saw both mine and Mitchell's name written on a board being held by a man in a suit. *Ah hell.* Of all the things I'd remembered to do, updating the honeymoon information hadn't been one of them.

I stepped toward the driver and smiled. "It's just me," I said, pointing at the sign. "Uh, the mister isn't coming."

His brow furrowed, and I could tell that he took what I had said all wrong. He thought I'd been dumped. Or worse, left at the altar.

He reached for a fresh flower lei and placed it around my neck. "For you. I'll throw his in the trash," he said, and I laughed.

"I'll go get my suitcase." I pulled at the lei around my neck and inhaled its scent before heading toward the proper belt, the air sweltering around me. I wasn't used to any kind of humidity really.

After managing to pull my bag off the conveyer belt, I lugged it toward the driver, who promptly took it from my hands.

"Is this your first time here?"

I smiled. "It is."

"Aloha. Welcome to Hawaii."

"Thank you," I said back, still smiling.

I couldn't believe that I was actually here. It had been a dream for so long, and now, it was coming true.

We walked across a busy street and into a parking lot.

Once I was in the backseat of the town car, the driver turned to me and asked, "Do you want to take the scenic route or the short route?"

I had no idea how to respond, so I asked, "What's the difference?"

"The short route goes right through the middle of the island. The scenic route takes us along the water the whole drive."

I still wasn't sure which one to choose. "Which would you pick?"

He chuckled softly, an accent permeating his words as he said, "Are you going to come back to Honolulu at all or stay on the North Shore?"

"I don't know," I answered honestly because I hadn't planned on coming here without Mitchell in the first place. All of my plans had included things to do in and around the resort and … in the bedroom.

"The scenic route," he said, choosing for me, and I nodded in agreement. "It'll take longer, but you're on Hawaiian time now."

"What's that mean?" I asked, fascinated that Hawaii apparently had its own way of living life that was totally different than anywhere else.

"You'll see soon enough, but basically, we don't rush. We take our time. You mainlanders go crazy about that, yeah?"

I actually understood what he was saying. "Yeah. We're always rushing from one place to the next."

"Can't rush here," he said with a hearty laugh.

We started driving, and I fired off a quick text to Dee, letting her know I had landed and was on my way to the resort, before putting my phone down and focusing on what was out my window. Aside from the tall buildings and what looked like a bustling downtown area, filled with colorful hotels, there were so many palm trees and a plethora of rolling green hills.

"It's so green," I said under my breath, but the driver heard me.

"It rains here every day."

"Every day?"

"Yeah, but it doesn't last. Usually only for, like, twenty minutes, and then it's gone." He snapped his fingers.

I realized that I was someplace unlike any other place I'd ever been before. Everywhere I looked, my eyes were met with more and more greenery, mixed with power lines draping across the roads, weighed down by branches or years of weather and wear.

I spent the drive staring out my window, trying to take non-blurry pictures with my cell phone as he pointed out places of interest, but nothing I took did any justice to what I was seeing with my two eyes. Oahu was stunning. The water was an incredible shade of blue, and there were so many things hidden beyond where the eye could see, just behind a group of trees or overgrown bushes. So much of the island felt isolated and almost empty, but I knew that wasn't the case.

We drove through a few small towns, each one teasing me into thinking we were almost at the resort. But before I knew it, we were isolated once more with nothing around us, except land and water. It continued that way until the driver took a right turn, and my senses were instantly overwhelmed. What had just been empty green hills and flat land was overtaken by a sprawling parking lot, adorned by a million palm trees, tennis courts, and scattered resort buildings that drew your eyes in.

I had no idea how close we were to the ocean, but the pictures online had shown the resort as basically being right on the sand.

"We're here." He pulled the car into the covered guest check-in area, where an attendant met us instantly.

They spoke to one another quickly and in a language I honestly wasn't sure I understood before the attendant was opening my door for me and taking my luggage from the trunk. I thanked my driver, gave him a cash tip, and followed the guy with my suitcase inside.

"I'll wait here with your things while you check in," he said, directing me toward the right counter.

But before I could even step that way, I noticed how beautiful it was all around me. I felt like I'd stepped into a surfer's paradise with boards used as decoration, gorgeous multicolored stone floors, and windows that faced the water. There was so much light in the room.

I took a few pictures with my phone and moved toward the check-in counter, where a sweet woman was watching me with a smile on her face.

"First time at the resort?" she asked, and I nodded. "First time in Hawaii?"

I nodded again.

"You're going to love it here. Can I get your name?"

Crap. What name did I make the reservation under?

"Spring Monroe. But it might be under Mitchell Flores," I said, hoping that if it was under Mitchell's name, they'd still let me check in. *What if I came all this way for nothing?*

"I see it. Both of your names are here. You have one of our ocean bungalows. They sit right on the water's edge. I see in the notes that you're celebrating your honeymoon?" she asked before looking past my shoulder and all around me, clearly in search of said husband.

"Solo trip. No Mr. Flores. Just me. I came alone." I was babbling and couldn't seem to stop.

Her face softened. "It happens more often than you'd think," she said, and I wasn't sure if she was trying to make me feel better or if it was the truth.

After giving her my credit card and letting her know I didn't have a car to park, she handed me the key card to my room along with a resort map. "Let me know if you need anything. We can help you book any excursions, or if there's anything you forgot to pack, just press zero on your phone," she said before adding, "Oh! You added The Club to your package. Sorry, I almost missed it."

"The Club?" I asked because I honestly couldn't remember everything that I'd done when I originally booked this trip.

"It's a private lounge. There's food in there and entertainment on the weekends. Your room key will give you access, and if there are any issues, the concierge there has your name."

"Okay. Sounds awesome. Thanks," I said with a smile and waited for her to basically excuse me or tell me I could leave.

I grabbed my waiting luggage from the guy who was still hanging back, holding on to it for me. I knew it was his job to bring it to my room, but that felt unnecessary. It was one suitcase, and it had wheels. Surely, I could manage it myself. Pulling out a few dollars, I handed them to him for his trouble.

I headed toward the main building's rear exit, not allowing myself to stop at any of the resort stores yet. There would be plenty of time for shopping later. A well-dressed man smiled at me as I neared him, and I almost tripped over my own two feet. I could tell by his attire that he worked at the resort, so I was sure he was only being pleasant in the way they had been trained to be, but damn, he was one good-looking man. Tall but not too tall with sun-kissed skin that looked like he lived outdoors. His hair was jet-black and cut so short that there wasn't even an option for styling it. I wanted to run my fingers across it, knowing that it would feel prickly against my skin but not hurt. His shoulders were broad, his biceps toned as they stretched against the fabric at his sleeves.

"Welcome to the resort, miss," he said with a smile as I went to pass him by.

I paused, my steps almost faltering. "Thank you," I said, but he didn't say anything else.

I thought he might offer to take my bag or something resort-like, but he stayed silent, so I walked away. But not without taking one last glance back at him. He was staring at me. Watching me even. And I had no idea why.

Once I stepped outside, into the air that no longer felt even remotely suffocating, I headed right toward the ocean, where my bungalow was waiting, my thoughts drifting for a second, back to the delicious guy. He hadn't given me a creepy feeling at all, but I glanced behind me again just to make sure he wasn't following me.

He wasn't.

So, why was I so disappointed by that fact?

I NOW LIVE AT THIS RESORT

SPRING

W HEN THE FRONT-DESK lady had said the bungalow was on the water's edge, she'd meant it. It sat right near the end of the land, facing the ocean from every direction, except the back. It was stunning, and I hadn't even gone inside yet.

Unlocking the door and stepping in, I noticed the roses, chocolate-covered strawberries, and champagne chilling on top of a beautiful wooden table. I wondered for a moment who might have sent it. Letting go of my suitcase, I walked toward the gorgeous display.

Mitchell didn't send this, did he?

That was when I noticed the note. Tearing it open, I pulled out the card. It was from the hotel, congratulating us on our wedding. With a cynical laugh, I uncorked the bottle and poured myself a tall glass. I could still celebrate.

"Here's to not making a mistake," I said out loud to absolutely no one and took a sip.

Oh, this is really good stuff.

I wondered for a second how I could incorporate that flavor into a frosting or a cake. Champagne cake with champagne frosting. My mind started spinning, and I ached to grab my notepad and a pen when I noticed the view. Floor-to-ceiling windows that looked out at the rocky cliffs and crashing waves below greeted me when I finally gave them my attention.

The view was mind-blowing. And oddly peaceful even though the ocean acted vengeful and angry at times. The waves came in, one right after the other, large, rolling, and punishing.

What is that? I wondered, craning my neck and trying to figure out what I was actually seeing in the distance.

Is that a group of seals swimming?

I stepped outside onto the lanai, passing by the table and two chairs as I kept my eyes focused on the ocean below.

No. Not seals.

Surfers.

A whole bunch of black wetsuits were paddling out into

the abyss, diving under the water before resurfacing, still clutching their surfboards against their chests. I stood there, fascinated by the way they navigated something so unpredictable. They saw motion in the water that only they could see, moving their arms rapidly before a wave even fully formed. I watched as they stood up on their boards like they were an extension of their legs and rode the wave all the way in before turning around and doing it all over again. It was bewitching.

Pulling my phone from my back pocket, I snapped a few pictures before texting them to Dee and my parents, letting them know I was safe and sound at the resort and would talk to them later. I sat down on one of the chairs and closed my eyes. As I breathed in long and slow, the sound of the ocean quickly turned into the soundtrack I wanted to define my life by.

I planned on never closing the back lanai door.

Does Oahu have bugs?

So far, I hadn't seen any, but that didn't mean I wouldn't wake up, covered in them, if I left my door open all night. Right? I made a mental note to ask someone but still didn't move from my spot even though I should have probably been unpacking and getting some food.

I MUST HAVE fallen asleep because the next time I opened my eyes, I was met with a darkening sky. I could see tiki torches lining the property in the distance, but I had definitely passed out. Glancing at my phone, I noticed two missed calls and a handful of text messages. Mitchell had sent one, and my heart sped up when I saw his name.

We hadn't talked much since the breakup, so it was an uncomfortable feeling when I pressed the message icon. He told me that he hoped the resort and Oahu was everything I'd always wanted it to be and to enjoy myself. It was a sweet message. Something he hadn't had to send, but I was thankful that he had.

I stood up from the chair and stretched my arms over my head as my neck and shoulders cracked. At least I hadn't slept through dinner. Stepping inside the room, I flipped on the lights and closed the door until I could find out about the bugs. Seeing my reflection in the mirror made me stop in my tracks. I looked awful.

I started laughing and shaking my head. My hair looked like birds had made a home in it, the humidity giving it volume and fullness it didn't have in Lake Bliss. I decided to hop in the shower, wash the travel grime off my body, and slip into a sundress for dinner at The Club. It seemed like the easiest option.

Twenty minutes later, I was heading out the door. When I found the secret entrance to The Club, I swiped my key card against the pad and waited for the door to unlatch. Pulling it open, I was met with a plethora of sounds, smells, and sights.

This room was incredible. Views of the setting sun lined an entire wall as soft music played from a live band. There was a full bar and multiple tables for dinner.

"Evening," a voice said, and I turned to focus on the guy greeting me, only slightly disappointed that it wasn't the man from earlier. "Will you be dining with us tonight or just hanging out?"

"Dining."

"Just one?" he asked before making a face that told me he probably shouldn't have asked the question that way.

"Yeah," I said as my mouth grimaced.

I'd thought it would be fine to travel alone, but everyone around me was partnered up. No one was here by themselves. It was awkward, to say the least.

He waved his arm and told me to sit wherever I wanted. I surveyed the room, looking for a table that would make me the most comfortable. When I spotted a two-person one in the corner, I made a beeline straight for it.

You can do this, Spring. It's just a meal. No one cares that you're here alone.

I felt a little childish and ridiculous. I owned my own business, for Pete's sake. I could eat a meal in a room filled with strangers by myself and survive it. And I was going to have to do it for the next nine days, so I might as well get used to it.

I looked up to see the sexy man from earlier looking around the room. When his eyes caught mine, a small grin appeared, and he headed in my direction.

There is zero chance this guy is going to walk right up and start talking to me, I thought to myself, but he did exactly that.

He stopped in front of my table, looking even better than he had when I first saw him. "Good evening," he said, and I noticed a small scar underneath his eye. I wanted to reach out and trace it with my fingertip.

"Good evening," I repeated as I started sweating underneath my dress even though the material was light and breathable.

This man made my heart rate speed up and my body turn to fire.

"Are you waiting for someone?" He looked down at the

seat across from mine.

"No," I answered, and I wondered what he might do next as he reached for the place settings on the table and started gently removing them without making a sound.

Oh my gosh. He worked here. He wasn't picking me out of the crowd to hit on me. He probably didn't even remember me from earlier this afternoon, and here I was, drooling over him when he was just doing his freaking job.

I was a disaster. I had no idea how single people did things anymore. I'd been out of the game for so long. No, that wasn't true. I'd never even been in the game in the first place. I was reading all the signs wrong, placing weight on a sexy smile and a friendly attitude when it was all part of his profession.

"Can I get you anything to drink?" he asked as he placed a menu in front of me. "This is our set menu for this evening. Please let me know if you any aversions or allergies."

"Um ..." I felt almost too dumb to speak, but I somehow found my words. "I'll take a mai tai?" I said it like it was a question.

"Are you asking me?"

I let out an uncomfortable laugh. "I have no idea what I'm doing. It's my first time here. I don't know what to order, but everyone said that mai tais are your signature drink?" Another question instead of a statement. I was on a roll tonight.

"They are one of them, yes. Do you like rum?"

"I do," I said as I nodded, and he grinned.

"Do you like sweet drinks?"

"Yeah."

"You'll like it then. I'll be right back."

He turned to head toward the bar, and I'd be lying if I said I didn't watch him walk away, my eyes zoning in on his butt before settling on those broad shoulders. His arm muscles were so big, and I wanted to reach out and touch them. Mitchell was good-looking, but this man was on another level of hot. They didn't make guys that looked like him in Lake Bliss.

I spotted him carrying what I assumed was my drink on a tray as he headed back toward the corner of the room, where I sat.

Placing the drink in front of me on the table, he asked, "Did you look at the menu?"

"Oh yeah. It looks great," I said, pushing the paper away from me and reaching for the drink instead. Grabbing the straw, I swirled the liquid around before taking a sip. Sugar and alcohol hit me all at once. "Oh, this is dangerous," I said with a laugh.

"Are you really here alone?" He looked like he couldn't believe it.

My eyes roved the room really quickly before landing back on his hazel ones and holding. "Is it really that hard to believe?"

"It's just that most people don't come to the island by themselves," he said as if he were an expert on what people did and didn't do.

I took another long swig of the drink before swallowing. "It was supposed to be my honeymoon," I started to say, and he gave me a knowing look. Before he could say anything in response, I made sure he knew the truth. "I called off the wedding."

His face morphed from sadness to surprised shock. "Really? And why was that?" he asked before pulling out the seat across from me and sitting down.

"Don't you have to work?" I asked, wondering if he'd get in trouble or fired for sitting with a guest instead of waiting on the other tables.

"My brother owns the resort. I was just helping out." He gave me a small shrug. "I didn't want to go home. You're my only table."

I wasn't sure what to make of that, but something he'd said struck me. "You didn't want to go home?"

He leaned back and let out a gruff laugh. "You first, sunshine. Why'd you call off the wedding?"

It was my turn to laugh. "I feel like that's a longer conversation than what I asked you."

"Fair," he agreed before blowing out a breath. "I live alone. But sometimes, I don't want to be alone."

His words settled somewhere inside of me. *He lived alone, but he didn't want to be alone.* Sadness was my innate response, but before I could ask him something else, he put up a hand.

"Now, give me the short version of why you called it off. Did you not love him anymore?"

"No." I shook my head. "I loved him. But I wasn't in love with him."

"What changed?" he asked, leaning forward on his elbows like he was genuinely interested in whatever had happened in my failed relationship.

"Nothing. Time? We'd been together since I was fifteen," I admitted to this perfect stranger, and instead of the conversation being unpleasant, it was comforting somehow.

"That's a long time. I mean, it's a long time when you're that young to start." He stumbled on his words, but I knew what he'd meant.

I continued drinking my drink, apparently way too fast

because all I tasted was the sugar and not really the alcohol.

"Slow down, girl, or I'll have to carry you back to your room."

"Oops," I said as I finished. "What's your name anyway?"

"Diego. And you are?"

I extended my hand toward him, and he grabbed it. His touch gave me goose bumps.

"Spring."

"Spring. I like it."

"Thanks. Are you from here?"

He nodded, that giant smile back. "Born and raised in the North Shore."

"Never leaving either, I bet," I added with a grin of my own. This place was beautiful, and I could see why people loved it.

"Don't plan on it," he answered, but there was sadness in his response. "Let me go check on your food."

He pushed the chair back and stood before I reached out and grabbed his hand, stopping him.

"Can you eat with me?" I asked before I knew what I was even doing.

Diego didn't respond, only walked away, so he shocked me when he reappeared, carrying two plates of food, two glasses of water, and two fresh drinks on a tray in his hands.

FALLING FOR A TOURIST

DIEGO

HAD NO idea what the hell I was doing. I didn't work at The Club. I had only stopped in to get some food to go when I saw Spring again and asked one of the servers if I could take her table. Not like they would ever tell me no—my brother really did own the resort. I'd seen Spring arrive earlier that afternoon, by herself, but I'd had no idea what her situation was up until a few minutes ago.

I hadn't been lying when I told her that most people didn't travel to the island alone. At least, not to Oahu. It was mostly couples and families that came here to vacation and explore all that our beautiful island had to offer. The more I thought about how I'd approached Spring without thinking, the more I realized that maybe I was running away from my issues.

Spring was a tourist. She would be leaving the island as quickly as she'd arrived on it. I had nothing to lose by spending time with her while she was here. We could give each other the things that we needed with no expectations. I wouldn't expect her to stay. And she wouldn't expect me to leave. It was a win-win situation.

I set the tray of food on top of the table before placing the plates in front of each of our seats. Handing her another drink, I warned, "Not so fast this time. They sneak up on you. And I brought you water. Hydrate."

She smiled as I essentially bossed her around, and it took everything in me not to lean across the table and claim that mouth with mine. Spring was sexy as hell, and the things I wanted to do to her body should be illegal—and probably were in some states. Not here though. I'd make sure of that. As long as she was willing, of course.

"Thanks. For eating with me," she said, her voice soft and kind.

It felt like it'd been forever since a woman had spoken to me with genuine kindness even though I knew that wasn't the truth.

"Was your breakup recent? Like, did you bail on him at your wedding, or did you split before the big day?" I asked, sounding like a dick but not at all meaning to.

"I wouldn't do that," she said as she took another drink of her second mai tai. "We broke up a couple months ago."

"And you didn't cancel the honeymoon?"

She slowly shook her head. "He told me that I should still come."

"Wow," I said, hoping I sounded as surprised as I felt. "That was"—I sucked in a breath—"generous."

"It was thoughtful." She replaced my word choice with one that obviously suited her situation better.

"I have a question that's none of my business," I started to say, and she smiled.

"But you're going to ask it anyway?"

I let out a laugh. "Yeah. Did you keep the ring?"

In my breakup, she'd kept the ring. I thought she should have given it back to me even though I sure as hell didn't want it, but still. Shouldn't she have at least offered? She hadn't. She'd kept it and most likely pawned it for cash after she bailed.

"I gave it back."

I felt a pang of jealousy zip through me. "That was the right thing to do," I said because I agreed with Spring returning it.

"I thought so too." She took a forkful of salmon and put

it in her mouth. "Oh, wow. This is the best salmon I've ever eaten."

"Yeah. The chef here is top-notch. He doesn't make a bad dish," I explained as I ate some of my own plate before it got too cold.

"You said your brother owns the resort?" she asked before taking a drink of her water.

"He does."

"But not you? Like, you're not a shareholder or part owner or anything like that?"

"Nope. I just help him out sometimes during the busy months," I said, and she took another bite of her food.

"Like now?"

"Exactly."

"So, what else do you do besides serve people food at The Club?"

She watched me, her eyes roving over my face, oscillating between my lips and my eyes. It only made me want to kiss her more.

"I give surf lessons and handle a few of the excursions."

"Do you like it?"

"I love it," I said honestly. "It keeps me busy."

I watched as her expression twisted a little and her eyes narrowed.

"So, when you're not working here for your brother, you're not working at all?"

I could tell that she wasn't trying to come off as rude. She was genuinely asking. It told me one of two things about her. Number one, she worked hard and most likely rarely took days off. And number two, she didn't respect laziness. I admired both of those qualities.

"I have my hands in a lot of different businesses these days," I said, evading the question a little bit because I wasn't quite ready to divulge my whole life story to her. She'd find out soon enough. Everyone always did. "What about you?"

Her face lit up, like she'd been waiting for me to ask this question forever even though we'd just officially met. "I own a bakery with my sister back home."

"And where is home?" I asked, taking another bite of food and a sip of my rum and Coke.

"It's a small town I'm sure you've never heard of, called Lake Bliss." She pursed her lips together as she waited for my response.

I slowly shook my head. "Nope. Where is it stateside?"

"Stateside?" she repeated with a laugh.

"Yeah. You're from the mainland. What part?"

"I love that you have your own language," she said with

a dreamy sigh before answering, "California."

"I like California," I said, thinking of all the times I'd been there, surfing.

"You've been?"

"A few times, yeah." I nodded. "So, this bakery," I said, wanting to change the subject back to her.

"Mmhmm?" She leaned forward, her eyes a little glassy, and I could tell that she had a buzz on.

"Tell me more about it."

"Okay." She grinned again before finishing off her drink and downing her water. "Um, my sister and I started Bliss Bakery about five years ago. She does all the marketing, and I create all of the flavors."

"You're the baker," I said, leaning back into my chair and folding my arms across my chest.

"Yep."

"And you love it?"

Her smile faltered for only a split second, but I caught it.

"I do," she said, but it was partially a lie.

"What aren't you telling me?"

"How'd you know?" she started to ask before stopping herself. "I guess it wouldn't hurt to tell you. Not like I'll ever see you again," she said, and for some reason, the words burned. Like a knife to the chest. "I love the bakery and what we built. I just don't know if I want to stay in Bliss forever."

Her words were familiar—too familiar—and they brought back a slew of memories I'd done my best to bury and never think about. But here they were, rearing their ugly head, all because her words had invited them to come out and play.

"Are you okay?" She reached out, her hand touching mine.

"Yeah. Sorry." I shook my head. "So, you don't want to stay in Bliss. Do you think that's why you broke up with your fiancé?" I was pushing the subject. Navigating the discussion in a direction that suited my own needs.

I'd had this conversation with my own fiancé before she left. Maybe if Spring gave me some insight, I'd understand Kaylee's mindset better. Take it less personal somehow. Be able to fucking heal once and for all.

"Wow," she said, almost like I'd struck her. Spring pulled her hand from mine and sat back, her fingertips pulling at her bottom lip. "You know, I've never thought about that before. Like, I'd never even put two and two together."

Her forehead creased like she was deep in thought. I knew I'd struck some kind of nerve, but she didn't seem upset about it. Matter of fact, she seemed the exact opposite.

"I'm sorry. I shouldn't have pushed," I said even though I really wasn't sorry.

"No, it's okay. It's a valid question and a really good point. I feel so stupid for not seeing it before. I think you're right though. If I had stayed with Mitchell, we never would have left."

"And you want to?" I asked her again.

She shrugged. "I don't know. But I think I'd like to have the option."

"And if you'd married this"—I swallowed—"Mitchell guy, you wouldn't have been able to do that?"

"He was going to take over his dad's company. And I had the bakery. How long until we had kids? I mean, no. Everything was set to follow this perfect path. That path did not lead out of Bliss. I've lived there my whole life."

"I've lived here my whole life," I said, feeling more than a little defensive even though Spring wasn't the cause of it. "And I don't want to leave. Ever."

"It's not the same thing," she said, her voice growing quiet.

"It is though. It's exactly the same thing."

"Diego," she said my name, and I stopped everything I had been doing and thinking and just focused on her. "I'm not sure why you're so mad right now."

"I'm sorry, Spring. I shouldn't have …" I couldn't even finish my thought before I was pushing away from the table, dropping my napkin on top of my plate, and practically sprinting out of there, ignoring the people calling my name.

WHAT THE HELL JUST HAPPENED?

SPRING

HAD NO idea what had just happened or why Diego was so upset, but he had run out of the room like his damn pants were on fire. Literally. He'd created a scene and left me sitting here, embarrassed. I felt like the whole room was watching me, like I'd done something wrong.

When a waitress came over, her eyes apologetic, I asked for a to-go box, so I could bring the uneaten food back to my bungalow. I was too mortified to stay. My mind kept going back and forth between the idea Diego had suggested about me not staying with Mitchell because I wanted the freedom to leave Bliss and him getting so freaking triggered by the conversation somehow.

The waitress reappeared. "Here you go. Don't mind

Diego. He's been a little off since Kaylee left him," she said.

I realized that I was probably supposed to know who Kaylee was and what she was referring to, so I nodded.

"Oh yeah. Of course. Thanks." I gave her a soft smile as her words settled into my bones.

He had been *off since Kaylee left him*.

Diego was suffering from a broken heart. How had I not seen it from a mile away?

I WOKE UP around six the next morning, my body used to only getting a handful of hours of sleep each night before heading to the bakery to create for the day. Stretching my arms over my head, the memory of last night's fiasco crashed back into me. Even though I'd done nothing wrong, I still felt bad, and for whatever reason, I wanted the chance to apologize to Diego.

What if I never saw him again? He didn't work here full-time or anything, so what if he did whatever he could to avoid me until I left? I hated the thought. It hurt me, knowing that Diego was in pain and that I'd somehow made it worse.

Rolling out of bed, I walked to the closet, where I'd

hung up my clothes, and reached for a sundress. Making my way to the dresser, I grabbed one of the multiple bathing suits I'd brought and changed into it before pulling the sundress over my head. Dressing in Hawaii was easy. And comfortable.

I needed coffee. Looking around the room, I noticed the coffeemaker but decided that it was never as good as someone else making it for you. They had to have the good stuff on the property somewhere, so I grabbed my room key and my cell phone and headed out the door.

The warm air hit me the second I stepped outside, and I stopped, breathing it in. I'd initially braced myself for there to be at least a slight morning chill in the air, but there was none. It was perfect. My flip-flops were loud against the cement walkway but soon drowned out by the sound of the crashing waves. Glancing at the ocean, I spotted a handful of surfers in there, doing their thing. The sun hadn't even fully risen yet, and they were already in the water.

I snapped a quick picture before a resort employee passed me by.

"Excuse me," I said, stopping him short.

"Aloha, miss. How can I help you?"

"Do you know where I can get some coffee?"

He laughed. "There's a shop inside the lobby. They're

local beans, grown here and everything," he said, the pride permeating his words.

Pineapples and sugarcane, before the mills got shut down, I was familiar with, but I hadn't even thought about them growing coffee on the island. But of course, they would. They had the perfect climate for it.

"That sounds perfect. Thank you."

We headed in opposite directions, and before I knew it, I was back inside the main lobby, this time paying a little more attention to my surroundings, taking it all in instead of focusing on Diego, standing all sexy in the distance like I'd done yesterday after checking in.

The walls were lined with black-and-white framed photographs of who I assumed were local surfers—some of them holding trophies, some of them simply catching the biggest waves I'd ever seen. A familiar smile stopped me in my path, and I moved toward the oversize framed photo, studying it before noticing the small inscription plate next to it on the wall.

Diego Peleke, North Shore local, wins first big title.

I knew it was him. I'd recognize that smile anywhere, apparently. He looked so young. And he was missing the scar that now lived underneath his eye.

Sucking in a quick breath, I smiled to myself before

snapping a picture of it on my phone. There was virtually no one in the lobby, so I didn't look like too much of a stalker.

"Coffee," I breathed out before turning on my heels and heading down the long entryway once more.

There was a cute resort shop that advertised local goods, surfboards, and clothes in their display window. It wasn't open yet, but I definitely wanted to go back in there and give them all my money. Spotting the coffee bar up ahead, I was thankful that there was no one in line. After ordering, I took my first sip and moaned out loud at the barista.

"This is heavenly," I said, and she smiled.

"It's because it's fresh. Local," she said, that pride beaming through her as well.

I smiled and walked away, coffee in hand, dead set on planting my butt on some of the rocks I'd seen that faced the surfers. Now that I knew Diego used to surf or maybe still did surf, I was even more enamored by them.

Once I found a giant rock to sit on and watch the water, I pulled out my phone once more and started snapping more pictures. Even though the surfers were pretty far away, I could still hear them laughing, shouting, and hollering from where I sat. They all sounded so happy, their voices echoing through the air.

After what felt like an hour of sitting in one place, I started wondering what I should do today. I hadn't booked any excursions prior to getting here, deciding to play it by ear once I was actually on the island and got a bit of a feel for it.

"I saw you taking pictures," Diego said.

I found myself suddenly nervous, like a kid who had gotten caught stealing cookies, as I whirled around on the rock to look at him, hovering above me.

"I …" I stumbled over my words. "I was."

"I know. Do you think I could see the ones you got of me?" he asked.

I'd had no idea that he'd been on the water with the others.

"You were out there? You'll be able to tell it's you? They're pretty far away," I attempted to explain, obviously nervous, but he only nodded and held out his hand for me to give him my phone.

I pulled up the gallery of pictures and handed it to him, completely trusting that he wasn't going to run off with it and never come back. He sat down next to me, his fingers quickly working on my screen, and before I knew it, he was handing my phone back to me.

"Thank you. I sent the ones of me to myself in a text.

And I put my number in your phone."

I cocked my head to the side, fighting back the grin that wanted to explode from forming. "Why would you do that?"

"I owe you an apology, Spring. For last night," he started, pushing up from the rock before shifting his weight from leg to leg. "I'm sorry I acted like that."

I stood up as well, reached out for his shoulder, and squeezed it. "I'm sorry if I said something that upset you."

He looked around, like he was gauging how many ears might be able to overhear us. And even though it was still early, people had finally gotten up and were milling around, claiming lounge chairs at the pool and seats at the unopen bar. Employees were hauling buckets of ice and wiping down last night's moisture from the tables, all within earshot of the two of us.

"You left your fiancé," he said point-blank, and it made it sound so much harsher, coming from his lips than it had felt in real life. Mostly because Mitchell had reluctantly agreed at first but eventually seemed okay with it all. "And my fiancée left me."

"Was it recent?" I had no idea why *that* was the first question that had popped into my head, but it was.

"About six months ago," he said, kicking at the pebbles

on the ground.

He said hello to the employees who passed us by, each one saying his name in greeting. It seemed like everyone knew him.

Six months, and he was still grieving the loss of her, of their relationship, of a future that no longer existed.

"Maybe you'll get back together?" I asked awkwardly. Why did everything I say to this man come out so stupidly?

He swallowed hard, his eyes moving from the ground to meet mine. "No. She's not coming back," he said, and my eyes grew wide, misinterpreting what he was saying. "No, no." His island accent drifted between us. "She didn't die. She just left the island."

"Ahhh," I said, as if understanding had finally dawned on me when it really didn't.

"You want to get out of here?" he asked, and before I knew what I was even agreeing to, I said yes.

We speed-walked through the lobby I'd been in earlier before I grabbed his hand and stopped him.

"That picture"—I pointed at the one I'd seen earlier—"it's you?"

"Yeah."

"You won something?"

He laughed, his eyes actually twinkling, like I was

insane. "Yeah, I won something," he said with an almost-wistful smile.

"You look so young. But you still look like you. Like, I knew it was you right away."

"I was only nineteen."

"No scar yet," I said, running a finger down my own cheek.

"No. That didn't happen for a few more years."

"How'd you get it?" I asked, clearly breaking through any personal boundaries he might have been trying to put up.

"I fell off my board. Went under and hit some coral. I'm lucky it didn't hit my eye," he said before looking around.

Everyone at the resort recognized him, making sure to greet him with alohas before carrying on with their duties. Being the brother of the resort owner sure seemed to have its perks.

"I like the scar," I said, and he grinned before taking my hand and leading me out of the resort and toward an old truck in the parking lot. "Is this the part where I leave with the hot guy and my body is never found again?"

"No. That happens much later in the story," he joked as he opened the door for me, and I hopped inside, having no idea where he was taking me or where we were headed.

I'VE LOST MY SENSES

DIEGO

I HAD SPRING in my truck and was currently heading toward my home near the Pipeline. A home I hadn't brought a girl to in six months. I wasn't sure why I wanted to explain things to Spring so badly, but I did. I wanted her to understand why I'd been such an asshole last night. And I didn't want her to hate me for it. A part of me figured she'd understand. Or maybe she could help me see why Kaylee had been so willing to walk away and leave.

Spring stared out her window, the ocean our constant as we drove the two-lane highway. "It's so pretty here. Do you ever get tired of it?"

"No. Never." And that was the truth. I loved living in the North Shore and never wanted to leave it. And that was exactly why Kaylee had. "What's Lake Bliss like?"

Spring laughed, and the sound filled up the whole cab of the truck. "It's kind of like this. I mean, not an island, obviously, but it has that small-town feel where everyone knows everyone else even though that's not really true."

"And you don't like it?"

She whipped her head toward me. "I love it. It's just that I'm not sure I want to live there forever, you know?"

I nodded slowly, my eyes focused on the winding road as we neared the exit for my house. "Yeah. You sound a lot like my ex." I hadn't meant for that to come off as offensive, but I had a feeling that it had.

"Tell me about her. What happened?"

"As soon as we park, okay?" I suggested, not wanting to start this conversation in the truck when we were so close to being home.

We drove into the hidden entrance and one-lane street, and I heard Spring gasp.

"Where are we going?" she asked as she took in the sheer size of the homes on the street.

"My house. I hope that's okay."

"You live here?"

She turned to me, her eyes wide, and I shrugged before pulling my beat-up truck into the driveway and cutting the engine.

"Home sweet home," I said.

"Is this a joke? You're joking, right?" she asked as she climbed out of the truck and headed toward the entrance.

I never forgot how beautiful my home was, but it was fun, seeing it for the first time through someone else's eyes. What had become everyday fixtures for me were brand-new to her. I watched as she ran her fingers across my old Buddha statue and bent down to inspect my koi fish swimming below it.

"You have koi fish? In a pond?" She shot me a look, her voice sounding almost childlike. "You have a pond!"

"I have a pond," I said, knowing that she was going to lose her ever-loving mind when she saw the rest of the house. If she thought the pond was impressive, wait until she saw the backyard. "Come on. They're not going anywhere." I reached for her hand, interlacing her fingers with mine like I'd done it a thousand times before, and led her to the front door, where I punched a code into the keypad.

Pushing the heavy wooden beast open, I held it for her as she started to walk through and stopped mid-step.

"Holy shit," she breathed out, and I started laughing. "Am I being punked?" She began looking around wildly, her eyes meeting mine.

"It's nice, right?"

"Nice?" she practically spat. "This isn't nice, Diego. This is"—she waved her hand in the air—"spectacular."

I carefully placed my hand on her lower back and gave her a little push as I led her toward the living room, which had views of the ocean and the pool from every window.

Spring cleared her throat. "You have a pond. And a pool. And the freaking ocean in your backyard."

I nodded. "I do."

"How? How can you afford this?" she asked before slapping her hand over her mouth. "I'm sorry. That was rude, but I'm confused. Are you rich?"

I laughed again. I'd almost forgotten that she had no idea who I was—or at least I'd assumed as much since I'd met her. She hadn't looked at me with any type of recognition at all. And when she'd asked about the picture of me on the resort wall, she still hadn't put the pieces together.

"Of course you're rich. Your brother owns the resort," she added softly to herself, but I heard her.

"Spring," I said her name to get her to focus her attention back on me. When her eyes met mine, I waved toward one of the private outdoor patios. "Want to sit outside?"

"God, yes." She jumped at the invitation.

I opened the patio door and led her outside, up the three

steps, and told her to take her pick. There was a four-person table and chair as well as two lounge chairs. I wasn't surprised when she picked the table, placing her cell phone on top of it.

"Would you like some food?"

She looked at me and nodded. "I am kind of hungry. I've only had coffee so far."

"I'll be right back," I said, and she stopped me.

"I can help."

"No. You sit. Relax."

"If you insist," she said before walking to the edge of the balcony and looking out at the water. "Diego?"

"Yeah?"

"Where are we exactly?"

"The Pipeline," I said before walking away, leaving her to soak in the information I'd just offered, wondering if she'd put it together on her own or if I'd have to fill her in. I assumed it was going to be the latter, which I didn't mind. I just hadn't had to do it in years.

Everyone on the island knew who I was. I was the hometown hero.

After putting a plate of various fruits, yogurts, crackers, and cheeses together, I headed back outdoors and deposited it all on the table. "Be right back. I ran out of hands," I said.

"Okay," she said as she took a piece of pineapple and put it in her mouth, stopping me from going anywhere.

I tried not to watch as her tongue darted out and licked her lips. They glistened in the sun from the juice of the fruit, and I wanted to lick it off, but I ran into the kitchen to grab a pitcher of water and two glasses before I did something rash like stripped her out of her clothes and fucked her on the table for anyone to see.

"Start talking," she directed once I reappeared, and I adjusted my shorts and cleared my throat.

I could have played dumb and pretended like I didn't know what she wanted to hear, but I was too old for that shit. "I used to be a professional surfer," I said as if that were something that everyone used to be at one point in their life.

"Oh." She looked at me with shock. "You surfed professionally? Like, you competed and stuff, and that was your job?"

God, she was adorable. So easily surprised, flustered, and cute.

"Yeah, Spring, it was my job."

"Wow. I had no idea that surfers made this kind of money."

I barked out a laugh. I couldn't help it. "Some do, but it's not common. Most of my money comes from endorsement deals and side hustles," I said with a grin.

"Side hustles. Like what?" She put her elbow on top of the table and placed her head on her fist as she batted those long lashes at me.

I could have lied or left things out or not told her anything else personal about me, but I didn't want to. Spring wasn't like the other girls who all knew who I was and where I had come from and wanted a piece of the fame that came with being associated with me. Even when I'd been with Kaylee, that hadn't stopped the groupies. Certain girls didn't care.

"I have a line of surfboards that I helped create. Some of them are in the store in the resort, but most are all over the islands," I said, and she sucked in a quick breath.

"I saw that store! I wanted to go in there this morning, but they were closed."

"Yeah. So, there's the surfboards, the pH-balanced line of Hawaiian island water, surf wax, and a clothing line for now."

"Wait." She put a hand up and giggled. "You have a line of water?"

"Don't knock it," I said, pouring her a glass from the pitcher. "Try it."

She took a long drink before wiping her lips with the

back of her hand. "It's tangy. Why is it tangy?"

"It's the pH balance. It's supposed to be better for you than regular water. I love it. I can totally taste the difference."

"I think it could grow on me," she said with a smile as she took another drink. "This whole place could grow on me."

I liked the sound of that. Too much. And the idea of it even more.

"Oh, wait. So, when you said we were at the Pipeline, you meant, the famous surfing spot?"

She was just now connecting all the dots.

"Yeah. The rest of the places down the sand are all team-sponsored houses. All the guys who surf professionally stay there with the rest of their teammates."

"Jeez," she said, sounding impressed. "Who knew that surfing was so badass?"

"Everyone but you, Spring."

"That's not fair. I bet my sister doesn't know."

"She might," I suggested with a grin.

"It's really beautiful here. Like, way prettier than I imagined or expected," she said. She moved from the table to one of the lounge chairs and lay down, her eyes closing. She looked so peaceful, lying there in the sun, her auburn hair soaking in the light. "Tell me what happened with Kaylee, Diego. Why'd she break up with you?"

She more than broke up with me, I thought to myself.

She'd broken off our engagement and called off our wedding and our life together.

I stood up from the table as well and sat down on the lounge chair next to Spring, scooting it close before opening the umbrella, creating some shade. "You'll get sunburned in ten minutes out here. I mean it."

"Oh." Her eyes popped open, and she tucked her legs into the shade I'd created with the umbrella. "Thanks for the tip."

I walked back to the table and grabbed our waters before sitting down, ready to get into it.

NO BOUNDARIES

SPRING

CONTINUED PUTTING my foot in my mouth whenever it came to Diego. I asked dumb questions, said stupid things out loud, and pushed him to tell me the kind of stuff I had no business pushing him to tell. But damn, I wanted to know. It was more than simple curiosity … even though I couldn't quite pinpoint what it was exactly.

"I'm sorry, Diego. You obviously don't have to tell me anything about Kaylee."

"No, I want to," he said, and I was a little shocked that he'd given in so easily.

Also, can we talk about this freaking mansion on the sand?!

"So, what happened?"

"We'd been together since high school," he started, and I felt myself smiling at the similarities between our two relationships. "Like you and Mitchell, it sounds like. But we were both juniors. I was already surfing then and planning on entering the pros when I turned eighteen."

"Is that how old you have to be?"

"Yeah. But I was competing locally long before that, and sponsors were already trying to court me. You know," he said, but I didn't know. Not really. I only imagined that it had to be like any other professional athlete.

"She didn't like that you were going to go pro?" I interrupted, assuming that maybe his ex couldn't handle the fame or the lifestyle.

"No. She loved it. She was really supportive. Never made me choose between her or the water. Never made me feel bad for how much I worked out or how often I watched reels of myself so I could get better," he explained, and I realized how little I knew about surfing or what it took to be great at it.

I stayed quiet, sick of asking all the wrong things. Plus, I could see the wheels spinning in his head. I could tell that this still hurt his heart, and it made mine ache for him. I wanted to take away his pain. I didn't want him to think about her when I was sitting right here.

"Once I went pro, I started traveling all over the world, competing, you know?" he asked, and I nodded like I knew exactly what he meant.

"Did she go with you?"

His face actually lit up when I asked that question, and jealousy burned through me. I was sick and twisted to even remotely feel like that when all he was doing was telling me what I'd been dying to know in the first place.

"She almost always came with me."

"That must have been nice," I said through gritted teeth like a freaking psychopath.

We both had history with other people, so why was I acting like his was some sort of competition against me?

"It was. At first," he said, and I sucked in a breath. "I bought this house not too long ago. We barely even lived in it together."

It hit me then. That he'd shared this place with another woman. He'd probably bought it with her in mind. But then again, Mitchell had built me a freaking house with his own two hands, and he was going to eventually share that with someone else. Someone who wasn't me. I needed to get past this nonsense.

"But I bought it to be our home base. No matter how much I traveled, I always wanted to have a home here."

"That makes sense."

"Kaylee liked the idea too. But she liked the idea of traveling more." He shook his head, almost as if he was arguing with himself inside of it. "See, the more places we went, the less she missed home. And the more places we went, the more homesick I got."

Everything hit me all at once. What had happened last night. How what I'd said about not wanting to stay in Lake Bliss struck a chord with him so deep that he had to get away from me.

"She didn't want to live here anymore?"

He shook his head. "There are two kinds of people on the island, Spring. The ones who never want to leave and the ones who can't wait to get away. The island becomes too small for some people. They want more. Or they want a better life."

"A better life how?" I asked, confused. What could be better than living in this paradise?

"It's really expensive here. Most people have to work more than one job. And most families have multiple family members living in their homes."

"I didn't realize."

"How could you?" he asked gently.

"Kaylee wanted a different life then?" I asked, steering

the subject back to her even though I knew it was hurting him. "I mean, not necessarily a better life. Just a different one?"

He sucked in an audible breath before drinking some of his tangy water. "I guess you could say that, yeah. She didn't want to settle down here and be stuck. And once I retired from surfing, she knew I'd never leave."

I put my hand in the air. "Okay, okay. When did you retire?"

"A little over a year ago."

"But she didn't break up with you right away?" I asked before realizing what must have happened. "You hadn't proposed yet," I breathed out, mostly saying the words to myself.

"Bingo." He pointed a finger at me. "I proposed, and she said she needed to think about it."

"Damn. That's harsh."

"I knew it was over then. Even before she said it. But to be honest, I think …" His eyes squinted as he contemplated his next statement. "I think I proposed so that she'd want to stay. I'd been slowly losing her for years, you know?"

"I think I know what you mean."

"Somewhere along the way, we stopped wanting the same things," he said, and I nodded.

"That's easy to do when you get together as kids," I said, but he didn't seem convinced. "I mean, it's easy to say you want this and that when you're seventeen and you haven't really lived life or figured out who you are as a person. I think it's easy to grow apart as a couple at the same time you're finding yourself as an individual. Does that make any sense?"

"Is that what happened to you?"

Oh. It was apparently my turn on the hot seat.

"I don't think so. I mean, neither one of us has really changed. I just stopped wanting where we were headed. But there was no real reason why," I tried to explain, but I was no closer to an explanation today as I'd been when I broke up with Mitchell.

"Was he mad?"

"At first. But his anger didn't last," I said with a light laugh. "He agreed. He's already dating, so he's not too broken up about it."

"Kaylee's dating too," he said before looking away from me.

"How do you know?"

"I don't want to tell you."

"Well, now, you have to," I said with a giggle before jumping over to his lounge chair and attempting to tickle his ribs. I had no idea what had prompted me to do that, but I was straddling him, staring down at his gorgeous face.

His hands grabbed mine, stopping my attack before he reached for the back of my neck and pulled me down to him. His mouth was instantly on mine, his tongue pressing against my own as I lost all track of any and every single thing and dived headfirst into that kiss.

Diego's mouth was hot, his tongue erotic, and it sent chills down my spine and woke my pussy right up. I'd never kissed anyone other than Mitchell before. God, I was so inexperienced. His fingers splayed across my back, pulling me harder against his body, and I swore that my body reacted to every single touch. I felt him everywhere, my inner thighs heating with friction as I started to grind against him without thinking.

"Damn, Spring," he breathed against me before forcefully separating our mouths.

I sat up, still straddling him, and he laid his head down on my chest.

"I haven't been with anyone, except Kaylee."

I swallowed hard, my lips already feeling thicker than usual. "I haven't been with anyone other than Mitchell."

He let out a soft laugh. "Aren't we a pair?" When I said nothing in response, except offering him a soft smile of my own, he added, "I didn't bring you here for this."

"I didn't think you did," I said quickly, hoping to reassure him.

I hadn't even remotely thought that Diego was trying to get me into bed. It was interesting how similar our stories were though. The way our former relationships seemed to almost mirror each other's.

"But now, I want to." He leaned up again, grabbing me once more as he started kissing my lips before moving lower.

I felt like I was being marked. Claimed. Possessed. And I loved it.

"Tell me you want this?" he demanded, but it was a question.

I knew he wouldn't go any further without my permission.

"I want this. I want you," I said, staring right into his eyes so there would be no mistaking my intentions.

He gripped my waist and lifted me off of him like it took no effort before pushing himself to a stand and attempting to adjust the massive hard-on jutting out from behind his shorts. I tried not to stare at it, but I was enamored.

"Hey, D! Yo, Kaylee, are you back?"

I felt my body go stick straight. Did I look like his ex?

A guy with a surfboard came jogging up toward the back of Diego's house. "Oh. My bad. You're not K. Sorry, bro," he said, and Diego walked over toward the side, reached down, and shook his hand.

"It's all good. Talk later, yeah?"

"Yeah," the surfer said before jogging away.

Diego stepped back toward me, apologizing, "I'm sorry. That was awkward."

"Do I look like her?" I asked.

He shook his head. "No. Just the hair, I think. It's the same color, you know? Boys are stupid."

I laughed and felt my body relax. "Where were we?"

A smile appeared, making his scar practically disappear from his face. "I was just about to take you upstairs."

"Don't let me stop you," I said, feeling bold, empowered, and suddenly adventurous.

Diego grabbed my hand and slapped my ass before leading me through his massive house, up the stairs, and into his bedroom.

REALLY DOING THIS

DIEGO

"**T**HIS IS YOUR bedroom?" Spring said.

Again, I'd forgotten that she'd never been here before. I'd have to let her go for a few seconds, so she could take a look around.

"Jeez, Diego, this is like a five-star resort. Nicer than your brother's hotel. Don't tell him I said that." She pressed a finger to her lips, as if it would be our little secret.

"Okay, you've seen enough. You can look after."

"After what?" She gave me a devilish smirk, and it took everything in me not to throw her on the bed and have my way with her.

"After I make sure you can't walk straight for the rest of your trip," I said, and her mouth opened in shock.

"Damn. Keep talking like that, and I might never leave," she said, and something inside me bent.

What if I wanted that?

I hadn't been lying when I said I hadn't been with anyone, except Kaylee. In the past, it had made me feel a little inadequate. But now, being here with Spring, I didn't feel so abnormal. Not to mention the fact that I hadn't even been remotely ready to take this step before ... well ... right now. Once I was inside of Spring, there'd be no turning back. No erasing what we'd done. Kaylee wouldn't be the last person I had been with.

"Hey. Are you okay?"

I turned to see Spring watching me, her eyes pulled together.

"Yeah. You?"

She nodded her head. "Surprisingly," she said before pausing for a breath and taking a step toward me, "I am. I want to do this. With you."

Her eyes told a story I wished I could read, but I got the gist. She meant what she said.

I finished closing the distance between us and kissed her softly at first before completely claiming her mouth. It belonged to me now. For as long as Spring was here, she was mine.

A low moan escaped as I worked my way down her neck and easily lifted the sundress off of her body. She was wearing a skimpy bikini underneath that no one should have the privilege to see her in, except me.

"You were going to wear this in public?"

She let out an uncomfortable sound. "Uh, yeah. What's wrong with it?" She stepped away from me and looked down.

"Only the fact that every guy at the resort would be imagining fucking you."

Spring waved me off as she let out a loud laugh. "You're insane."

"You clearly don't know how hot you are," I argued.

"I brought, like, six other suits," she said, as if that made it better.

If I knew women, I knew that all her suits were most likely the same.

"Do they all look like this?" I spun her around to see that her bottoms were basically a thong and half of her perfectly peachy ass showed.

She shrugged. "Kind of? But if it makes you feel any better, I don't plan on fucking anyone but you while I'm here."

It should have made me feel better. It should have made

me feel a million things, but somehow, it kind of made it worse. Because her being here was temporary. She'd leave and never look back, just like Kaylee had done.

"Damn right you won't," I growled before untying the strings on her bikini and watching it fall to the floor.

Grabbing her body, I lifted her up and set her on top of the bed before I took her in. She looked so beautiful, naked.

I hovered over her, putting my weight on my arms until my shoulders burned but I didn't give a shit. They could give out for all I cared, I was going to take my time with her and devour every inch of her precious body. Pressing my lips to her neck, I nibbled and sucked before letting my tongue trace the curves of her collarbone. I continued licking my way down, her hands already fisting my head as I reached the full mound of one of her perfect tits.

Taking the nipple into my mouth, I sucked at it before flicking it with my tongue, making her body arch off the bed.

"You like that?" I asked even though her body told me everything I needed to know.

"Yes. Oh my God, don't stop. And don't forget the other one," she said, her voice all breathless and heady.

I did as she'd directed, moving to her other tit and taking it in my mouth, sucking and biting like I'd never get enough of doing it. The salt on her skin was my aphrodisiac, and the more her hips bucked against me, the harder I sucked.

My eyes moved from her chest to her face. Her head was thrown back, eyes closed, and I reached up to touch her cheek with one hand. She opened her eyes then, all of her hazel irises crashing into my green ones. I made sure she was still watching as I lowered myself off of the bed, grabbing her legs and pulling her with me until I could easily reach her while on my knees, her legs wrapped around my shoulders.

She licked her lips, her eyes growing wild as she waited for what she knew was coming next. I teased her first, kissing the inside of one thigh before doing the same to the other.

"Stop tormenting me," she breathed out, and I chuckled against her skin before diving in.

My nose hit her clit as my tongue licked at her opening, the taste of her totally different from how Kaylee used to taste. I ate her pussy like she might take it away from me, my tongue fucking her hole before moving to her clit and sucking on it, making her squirm like crazy against me. I pressed two fingers inside and twisted, making sure I hit her G-spot before playing with her clit some more.

"Holy fuck, Diego. What are you doing right now?" She

sounded so out of breath, so consumed with lust that I wasn't sure if it was a compliment or if she was genuinely asking.

To answer would have meant stopping, and I sure as hell wasn't planning on doing that. I continued fucking her with my fingers as I started eating her faster, my tongue lapping her up as quick as I could. I felt her start to quiver, her insides gripping and pulsating on my two fingers, and I knew she was close to releasing.

"Oh God, don't stop. Don't stop eating me. Just like that," she said, and I went fucking crazy with her words, licking and finger-fucking and sucking her pussy until she came, her body violently shaking and trembling in the aftermath.

I maneuvered myself out of her legs and pushed to a stand, wiping at my mouth with the back of my hand. She looked almost embarrassed, her cheeks pink as she watched me.

"I don't normally talk like that." She slapped a hand over her mouth, and I gave her a sly grin.

"Well, I liked it." I bent down and kissed her hard, making sure she tasted herself on my tongue. I'd figured she might pull away, but she didn't. She took my kiss and matched it, wanting more.

"Your turn," she said, and I wasn't sure what she meant until she got off the bed and reached for my shorts, pulling them all the way down.

"If you insist," I managed to mutter out because no guy in their right mind turned down a blow job from a beautiful woman he planned on sleeping with shortly thereafter.

Her hand fisted the length of me while her other one worked my balls between her fingers. All at once, her mouth was on me, hot and wet, taking me in. I reached out to grip something, but there was nothing there. I was lucky I didn't fall right down. This felt so fucking good.

"You feel amazing," I said, making sure she knew that I liked what she was doing.

I looked toward the floor and watched as her head bobbed on my cock like it was the greatest lollipop she'd ever had in her mouth. She kept sucking me, her hand moving at the base of my dick as she looked up at me, her expression turning me even more on. If she kept working my dick like that, I was going to blow it and then need time to recover before being inside her.

What if I lost the chance? What if she changed her mind between now and then?

Reaching for her shoulders, I pulled her body, and she released my dick with a loud pop.

"Why'd you stop me?" she asked before her eyes narrowed. "It wasn't good?"

"Spring, it was amazing. I just couldn't hold out any longer, and I really want to be inside you."

Her expression softened instantly with my words as she moved herself back on top of my bed and extended her hand out for me to take. She pulled me down, kissing me sweetly, and I moved to grab a condom from my nightstand before rolling it on. I pushed myself inside of her without easing into it, going slow, or even warning her. She gasped before adjusting her hips, throwing her legs back, allowing me to fuck her even deeper.

This woman was made for me, I thought as I took her, my body fitting with hers like two puzzle pieces that only worked together.

DIEGO IS A GOD

SPRING

W E CAME TOGETHER.

As in simultaneously.

At the same time.

Two strangers who had never been together sexually didn't normally do that. But then again, he hadn't felt like a stranger while I had his dick in my mouth. Or while he was inside of me. Our bodies had moved together like we'd been doing it for years.

And as the two of us lay side by side in his bed, desperately trying to catch our breath, I tried to make those thoughts leave my head. Just how comfortable it had been with him. I figured it should have been at least a little awkward, but we had fallen into a pace and rhythm that needed no explanation or help.

"That was incredible," he said, his chest still rising and falling in rapid succession—I could see it out of the corner of my eye.

"It was," I agreed, turning my head to look at all of his gorgeous tanned glory. Apparently, surfing did a body good.

He angled toward me, his hand reaching out to draw lazy circles on my stomach. "You don't regret it, do you?" he asked, and I felt myself panic.

"Not at all. Do you?" I asked because maybe he did but was too afraid to say it.

"No. I thought it would be weird, but it wasn't."

I felt myself smile. "I thought the same thing."

"Spring?" he said my name like a question, his hazel eyes staring deeply into mine.

"Yeah?"

"You don't feel like a stranger," was all he said before leaning forward and kissing me softly.

When he pulled away, breaking the kiss, I reached out, my hand cupping his cheek. "You don't either. I'm oddly comfortable with you."

He nodded at my words, and I knew he felt the same way. There was something between us that we couldn't explain. Maybe it was our shared history with relationships. Or maybe it was something deeper than there were words for. I wasn't sure, but I was content with simply accepting whatever was happening between us. It was only temporary anyway. Maybe we both needed exactly this, and we were lucky enough to find it in each other.

"You know," I started to say, and he focused his attention back on me, "don't think I forgot."

"Forgot what?"

I grinned and bit my bottom lip. "How you knew Kaylee was dating."

He blew out a breath and pretended to be embarrassed. "Dang it, Spring," he said before sitting up.

I followed his posture, propping a few pillows behind my back for support. "Spill."

"It's not that big of a mystery. I mean, I'm sure you could narrow it down."

"Why are you making this so hard?" I teased. "So, you still stalk your ex on social media. We all do it."

His face paled slightly. "See? I knew you'd figure it out."

He sounded so … something—I wasn't sure what it was.

"You had no idea she'd moved on?"

"No. Not until I saw her posts of them together."

"You don't know him, do you?" I asked, realizing that if she'd started dating one of his surf buddies or someone from his industry, it would be like another knife to the heart.

"No. Apparently, he's some rich dude from San Diego who does a lot of international travel. It's exactly what she wanted, so I hope she's happy."

"Do you really mean that?"

His eyes shot to mine. "Of course I do. I mean, it hurt like hell at first to know that she was basically choosing travel over me, but—"

I put my hand up to stop him. "She wasn't choosing travel over you, Diego. She was choosing herself. And I don't know if that makes it any better, but she did the right thing. If she had stayed with you and become miserable at some point, she would have left eventually. And it would have been harder and hurt more."

I was clearly projecting my own feelings onto Diego's story. And I knew that I was completely speaking out of turn for a woman I knew nothing about, but in my mind, it made perfect sense. I got why she'd left. I felt like I understood her desire to choose herself over everyone else. If you didn't choose you, who else would?

He blew out a soft breath, and I wondered if I should

apologize for saying all of that. "You're right. Thank you. I guess I never expected her to really leave. Even though she'd been saying it for years."

"I'm sure you were focused on your career. Why'd you retire anyway? Is that too personal?"

He grabbed my hand, brought it to his lips, and kissed my knuckles. "No, babe. Not too personal. I got in a bad accident, where I got the scar you asked about. I was unconscious. Almost drowned. They had a hard time finding me at first because my leash was tangled, holding me under. They had to cut me free."

I swallowed hard, my throat suddenly thick as I worried for the man I hadn't even known then. "That's terrifying."

"I took some time off to recover. I'd broken my hand with the fall somehow. Had two broken ribs from where my board had hit me. I'd been thinking about retiring for a little bit by then, and it just seemed like the perfect time."

"Can you go back if you want? Like, do you miss it?"

"Yes, and no. I miss competing but not being gone all the time. I like feeling settled. I like being home. I'd been traveling nonstop for seven years. It takes a toll mentally and emotionally, you know? It gets old," he admitted.

I could see why it hadn't worked out between him and his ex. For her, it hadn't grown old. It had only gotten more exciting and inviting.

"Are your parents still here on the island?" I asked, and he nodded.

"They are, but they're not here now. They leave for two months every year and go visit my aunt and uncle on the mainland."

"The same two months every year?"

"Yeah. When all the tourists come, they go," he said with a laugh as my stomach growled. "Ah, I hear you, little tummy." He pressed his ear against my exposed stomach. "Let's go feed you." He planted a kiss there and stepped out of bed, reaching for my hands to help pull me up.

Grabbing his shorts, he pulled them on before reaching for my bathing suit and giving it a dirty look. "Not sure I should give this back to you," he teased.

I reached for it, but he pulled it away from my grasp.

"I guess I could just go out there naked."

"Here!" He threw it at me, and I laughed while I slipped it back on but left my sundress on the floor for now.

I followed him back down the stairs and through more of the house I hadn't seen before.

"This place is really incredible," I said as I stared at the art on the wall before noticing the pool.

"You really like it?"

I shot him a look. "Who wouldn't?" I asked before a thought struck me. *Did Kaylee not like this house?* I couldn't imagine anyone not enjoying this view and luxury. It was oversize, huge even, but still felt comfortable and homey. Something I appreciated.

Before I knew it, we were back in the kitchen, pulling out more food from the fridge. It was fully stocked with everything a person could possibly want or need.

"Want to sit by the pool or the ocean?"

I started laughing, and he stared at me like I was off my rocker.

"Pool or ocean view, madam? How could I go wrong with either?"

"The pool has more privacy," he said with a wink.

"Pool it is!" I held my hand in the air because if he wanted to ravage my body again, I was going to allow him … willingly … and privately … by the pool.

Once we were outside, there were so many options to choose from. Did we want to lie next to the pool, under the covered patio, or sit underneath one of the many palm trees? I chose the covered patio to start, and Diego followed my lead. We both sat down, and I reached for a sandwich he had brought out, taking a giant bite.

"Do you have to work later?"

"I worked this morning."

"You did?"

"Early surf lessons," he explained, and I formed an O with my lips, not realizing that he had been teaching anyone when I saw him.

How had that only been earlier today? It felt like days ago.

"Do I get to meet your brother?" I asked without thinking about how insane that might have sounded.

His eyes shot up, and he gave me a smirk. "Do you want to meet my brother?"

"I kinda do. Is that weird?"

"Not weird."

It was definitely weird. Or at least, it should have been. But for whatever reason, it wasn't.

Why isn't it? Why does everything feel so natural with him?

"It's a little weird," I objected, wanting him to admit that this thing between us should have been at least a little odd.

"Fine. It should be, but it's not. This should feel weird and awkward, and I should be driving you back home instead of making you lunch, hoping you'll stay for dinner," he said all in one breath, and I had no idea which thought to start focusing on first.

My mouth slowed down its chewing until it was practically nonexistent. The food sat in my mouth before I forced myself to swallow it. A slew of emotions ran through me, all of them positive.

"Did I scare you off?" Diego bent his head lower as he looked at me through concerned eyes.

"No," I admitted. "The opposite, I think."

A small smile formed. "I made you want to stay for dinner then?"

"You made me want to check out of the resort and stay here with you instead." I laughed, but I wasn't entirely joking.

"That can be arranged." He was dead serious. The look in his eyes and the tone of his voice let me know that he meant it.

"I shouldn't," I started to argue before speaking my thoughts out loud, "Right? That would be insane."

He pushed out of his chair and walked to me, dropping to his knees, taking my hands in his. "This whole thing is crazy. I've never done anything like this before. I've never wanted to, but with you, it's different. Don't ask me to give you reasons why because I won't be able to."

I watched his mouth move with his words, stared at the

details of his face the fullness of his lips, the scar on his face, the hazel flecks shining in his eyes. This man was a god, and I wanted to worship at his feet for the next week.

"You can keep your room at the resort, but it seems unnecessary."

"Why's that?" I asked with a smirk of my own.

"Because after today, there's not a chance in hell I'm letting you go to sleep each night without me by your side."

Well.

Damn.

I think that's the sexiest thing any guy has ever said to me.

"That was hot," I said, practically breathless and ready to have him inside me again.

"Let's go pack your things then," he suggested, and chills raced through me.

I was suddenly nervous. More nervous than I'd been so far with him.

Could I really check out of the resort and stay here with him? It was too big of an ask. Too fast. Plus, I wanted to eat at the restaurants there, hang out by the pool, and have drinks with large pieces of fruit in them. I really did want to do all of those things, but they felt like weak excuses.

"How about we start with an overnight bag?" I

suggested, and he stood up, taking me with him.

Diego pulled me into his arms and hugged me. It felt so good, being pressed against him like that, my skin buzzing just from being near his.

He continued to hold me as he kissed the top of my head. "Let's go get that bag."

HAVE I LOST MY MIND?

DIEGO

HALF-WONDERED WHAT the hell I had been thinking when I told Spring to check out of the resort and stay with me, but I'd meant it. I still meant it. I wanted her here when I went to bed at night and when I opened my eyes in the morning. I had no idea what the hell that meant, but I wasn't going to start analyzing it now. She didn't live here. She would be leaving soon, and I had to keep that thought front and center in my mind. Even though I knew it was too late for being rational, I was caught up in this girl.

We were back in my truck, navigating the roads toward the resort, my hand holding hers, and I realized how … *content* I felt. A feeling that I'd been lacking for months now, maybe longer, was suddenly overwhelming me. I was happy. Whole.

And it was all because of her.

Pulling into the employee parking lot, I cut the engine and hopped out before opening Spring's door for her. She smiled, her body falling into mine as we walked in perfect rhythm, like we'd been doing it all our lives.

"Should I …" She dropped my hand and made a face. "Since everyone here knows you?"

I hadn't thought that far ahead. Part of me wanted to show her off to the world, but another part of me knew that this would cause an insane amount of gossip and island talking.

"I hate to say yes, but let's just"—I searched for the right words that wouldn't hurt her feelings—"play it casual for right now."

"Sure," she agreed. "But people will see us leave together, I'm sure."

"I know. I don't care if they see us leave. That way, they can talk about us after we're gone, not while we're still here."

It made perfect sense to me. And I think she understood where I was coming from.

We walked around the grounds, avoiding the main lobby, as I fired off a text to my brother, asking if he was here or not.

"Is that a horse stable?" she asked, and I realized that I'd basically stolen her vacation from her. She hadn't seen anything on the property yet.

"Yeah. Want to see it?"

"Yes!" she exclaimed, sounding so happy, and I planned to make sure to take her riding while she was here.

The horses were outside, grazing as we approached, and I was thankful they hadn't been put away already. Sometimes, the weather was unpredictable and made the horses skittish. My phone vibrated in my pocket, and I fished it out, seeing my brother's name on the screen.

I answered it. "Aloha, brother."

He asked me where I was, saying he'd be right out before ending the call.

I turned to look at Spring. "My brother's coming out to meet us."

"Oh." She looked down at her sundress and back up at me.

"You look beautiful," I said, and she blushed.

"What's he like?"

"Professional," was the first word that came to mind before another. "Serious."

Samson was my polar opposite. Where he excelled, I

struggled. And vice versa. He couldn't catch a wave if I paid him to do it. It was almost unbelievable that we had the exact same parents.

"Is he nice?"

"Very."

"Judgmental?"

"No. But he's never seen me with anyone other than Kaylee, so he might be a little taken aback," I explained honestly.

"Is he married?"

"Yes. And they have two kids."

"Okay." She slapped her hands together, seemingly satisfied with the lowdown I'd given her. It was cute, the way she needed to be prepped, the information she wanted.

"Any more questions? Because that's him." I pointed to the man in the suit heading our way.

Spring bounced back and forth on the balls of her feet as Samson approached, a giant grin on his face before he took Spring in and gave me a look.

"Brother," he said, greeting me with a hug and a slap on the back. "Who's this?"

I stepped to the side. "This is Spring. Spring, this is my brother, Samson."

She reached out her hand, and Samson took it, giving

her a firm shake.

"It's nice to meet you. The resort is breathtaking," she said, and his face lit up with pride. She knew the way to his heart—complimenting him on his business.

Samson gave me a quick, curious look before refocusing on Spring. "Are you a guest here?"

She nodded. "I am. I'm staying in one of the bungalows. Beautifully decorated, by the way. Incredible views."

"Thank you," he said sincerely before looking at me. "So, you're stealing one of my guests from me then?"

I choked out a laugh. "I'm trying."

Samson put a finger to his lips and shook his head. "Interesting. Very interesting, little brother."

"I told you he'd be weird about it," I said toward Spring, and she giggled.

She smacked my shoulder, and I took the opportunity to grab her and hold her in my arms.

"You did not," she disagreed. "He didn't say that."

My brother couldn't hide his surprise, his shock, or whatever else was floating around in that big head of his. "Should I take you off the schedule for the rest of the week?" he asked.

I leaned down toward Spring and whispered in her ear.

She maneuvered out of my grip and turned to face me.

"It's up to you. But don't disappoint anyone who was excited to surf with you."

"Keep all my lessons, but if someone else can handle the excursions until Spring leaves, that would be chill."

"It's not an issue, bruh. You know that."

He was being so agreeable. Not that I'd really expected otherwise, but I never knew. This was his business, and I was potentially making it more difficult for him to run it effectively.

"I'd better get back though. It was nice to meet you, Spring. Talk to you later, Diego."

Once my brother left us alone, I really studied Spring's expression and body language.

"That was okay, right?"

"Yeah. He was nice."

"Can we go pack that bag now?" I said, realizing that I wanted her all to myself.

I didn't want to be at the resort anymore. I didn't care about people seeing us together or what they might say. I just knew that I wanted to be home, with her.

"You're so impatient," she teased. "I mean, we just got here. The least we could do is have a drink at the pool bar. I haven't done that yet."

"Okay, Spring, we can do that."

People on the island would hear about me and Spring soon enough, if they hadn't already, especially after last night. It wasn't enough that I'd sat down to eat with her, but I'd also walked out on her, too, leaving her there alone to pick up the pieces for prying eyes to see. There wasn't a chance in hell that the employees hadn't gone all apeshit over seeing me with someone who wasn't Kaylee.

I was honestly half-surprised my phone hadn't rung from Kaylee herself, calling to see if it was true or not. Then again, I hadn't reached out to her when I realized that she'd moved on. I wrote a novel of a text message that I eventually deleted and never sent. There was no point, I'd finally realized as my finger hovered over the Send button before pressing Delete instead.

She and I were over. Sleeping with Spring had definitely solidified that. Not in my mind, but in my heart.

So, if everyone was going to start talking about us, I'd give them something to talk about.

THE POOL BAR IS THE BEST BAR

SPRING

DIEGO AND I pulled up two barstools underneath the oversize cabana-inspired bar and sat down. I was surprised there were any seats available, to be honest. The pool was to our left, and the ocean was in front of us. It was almost as impressive as being at Diego's house but not quite. I realized in that moment that I enjoyed the privacy that his home had given us. While the resort was truly stunning, it was filled with strangers who were very invested in who I was there with.

As expected, everyone who worked there knew Diego by name. I didn't miss the way that the guys gave him head nods, showing their approval for whatever it was that he and I were doing. Nor did I miss the way all the females sized me up, not even hiding the fact that they were doing it. They weren't necessarily happy that I was hanging out with their hometown surf god. I was only a measly tourist after all, and if anyone should have been spending time with him, it clearly should have been one of the local girls.

"Babe," Diego said.

I flinched at the nickname, purely from surprise, not distaste. I actually found myself loving the way the endearment flew from his lips, meant for my ears.

"Uh-huh?" I asked, batting my lashes a few times more than necessary.

"Do you want me to choose for you, or do you want Jon here to make you something?"

"I'm Jon," the bartender said, his hair tucked back into a hat that bore the resort logo but nothing else he wore did. He looked so casual that I was surprised it was even allowed.

"I like your shirt. The logo is really cool," I said, never having seen it before, and Jon gave a howl.

"You're joking? She's funny," Jon said, and I looked at Diego, confusion written all over my face.

"No, bruh. She doesn't know. I mean, she knows, but she hasn't seen," Diego told him.

I was lost in their conversation. I had no idea what they

were talking about.

"That's your boy's shirt. It's his logo. His clothes." Jon pointed at Diego, and my mouth dropped open.

"Ah. I love it," I said again, turning to Diego and pressing a kiss to his lips, feeling so proud of what he had created, like I'd been a part of it somehow. "Shit. I'm sorry," I said before realizing that I'd kissed him in public with more eyes than I cared to count watching.

"Too late for that, babe," he said, grabbing my face and kissing me hard, deep, and with tongue for everyone to see.

If there had been any question about the two of us hooking up, there wasn't anymore.

He pulled away with a smile, and I felt the blush creep into my cheeks. I tried to steady my breath, but it was difficult. He made me breathless in the best possible way.

I looked between the two guys, feeling so at home that it was almost unnatural. Then, I turned to Diego and finally answered, "You choose for me. I trust you."

Diego laughed as he pointed at a drink on the menu that I couldn't see and Jon gave him an approving nod. I bounced on my seat, waiting for whatever concoction Jon was going to make for me when he returned quickly with a …

Piña colada?

"Is this a piña colada?" I asked, surprised that he'd get me something so traditional and simple.

"Yeah. But try it. We make the best ones on the island," Diego said.

I took a sip before the flavor exploded on my taste buds. My brain instantly, once again, wanted to create this flavor in a cake and frosting.

"The pool bar is always the best bar," Jon said, as if trying to stave off an argument that he wouldn't be getting from me.

"This is so good and so strong," I said, noticing the dark float of rum on top before I started mixing it.

"Three kinds of rum. That's what makes it so good. It's not too strong and not too sweet. It's the perfect blend," Jon mentioned with a shrug.

There was a huge slice of pineapple on the side of the plastic cup, and I removed it, taking a big bite. "This pineapple is unreal." I wiped at the juice I knew was dripping down my chin.

" 'Cause it's grown here," Diego said, and I wondered what other cake creations I could make, using all of the island's fresh ingredients.

Jon slid a glass of something toward Diego, and he took a drink.

"Perfect. Like always. Mahalo."

"Everyone's watching us," I said as I looked around, realizing that pairs of eyes were still practically glued to our backs.

"I know. I created a scene earlier by kissing you like that. Sorry."

"Don't be sorry. I'm not. I just want you to be okay. Comfortable." I struggled with the right words to express how I was feeling.

I cared about Diego, and I knew that this island was small in the same way that Lake Bliss was. Everyone was involved in your personal business, whether you wanted them to be or not. Not that we were helping the situation by kissing in public and whatnot. But still.

"I'm not uncomfortable," he said, throwing his arm around the back of my chair, his fingertips brushing my shoulder.

"Okay." I turned my head and pressed a kiss to his cheek. "Let me know if that changes."

"You're really something else," he said, and I took it as a compliment, assuming he meant it that way. "Thank you. For caring."

"You'd do the same for me," I said without a second thought, knowing that it was true.

We might have been strangers before, but we felt like anything but now. There was some innate knowledge going on between the two of us. Something connecting us beyond what could be explained. I wasn't sure that I believed in soul mates, but Diego had me questioning my thoughts on the matter. If soul mates truly existed, then he might be mine. It was the only thing that made any kind of sense.

"I would," he agreed.

I took another swig of my drink, trying not to down it too quickly but it was hard to drink it slow. It was just that delicious. "I can't believe how good this is," I said, finishing it off, and he laughed.

"You're going to be buzzed soon," he warned.

He whistled for Jon and gave him a hand signal that I assumed meant I was getting another one.

"I'm a fun drunk," I said confidently, straightening my back. "Not the crying, havoc-wreaking kind of drunk. I just get happier."

Diego blew out a breath of relief. "That's good to know. Kaylee was super dramatic. Always pushing me to get into fights," he said before wincing. "I'm sorry I keep bringing her up."

"It's okay. Really. It helps me understand you better. What your relationship was like. Where things went wrong.

I don't mind you talking about her," I tried to explain before my empty cup was replaced with a new one. "Unless you're still in love with her. I'm not sure I could handle hearing that right now."

It was a crap thing for me to demand of him—that he couldn't be in love with his ex-girlfriend anymore—and I knew I shouldn't have said it. But I wasn't sure I'd be able to leave and sleep with him again if he told me that he was.

"I still love her, Spring," he started to say, and I swore my heart dropped out of my chest. "But I'm not in love with her like I was. I care about her, and I will always want what's best for her, but I know that isn't me. She really hurt me when she chose to leave, but like I told you, I had known it was coming. I'd seen the signs for a long time. I just tried to pretend like they weren't there. And I proposed for all the wrong reasons because I'd been with her for so long. I didn't know how to be without her."

I understood exactly what he was saying because I felt the same way. His story was too similar to my own. "I get what you're saying. Completely."

"I know you do. That's part of the reason why this works so well between us." He pointed between my body and his own. "Part of the reason," he said again, and I softened.

"Let's finish these and get out of here."

"I have a better idea," he said as he stood up from his chair and reached for both of our cups. "Let's take these to your room."

"I like the way you think, sir."

"I figured you would."

We took the drinks to my bungalow and sat on the lanai, watching the ocean and listening to the waves before I started throwing some stuff together to bring to his house.

"Pack for more than one night, okay? I don't want you to be here when you could be with me."

I had disagreed about an hour earlier, but now, with the alcohol swimming in my veins and the public display we'd made at the bar, I was in no mood to argue. It seemed pointless. I knew in my gut that I'd be staying with him every single day and night until I left anyway.

"Fine." I pretended to relent to his demands, but I had planned on packing a little extra anyway, just in case. "Promise me one thing?"

"What's that?"

"We stop at the store, so I can bake for you. I haven't baked in days, and I'm going a little crazy, to be honest."

"You want to bake for me?" His eyes grew wide, and he wiped at his mouth as he pretended to drool.

"Yeah."

"You are the perfect woman. I mean, except for one thing," he said, and I thrust out my hip, placing a hand on it.

"Oh yeah? What's the one thing?"

"You don't live here."

Well, damn. There was that.

BAKING IS MY ZEN

SPRING

D IEGO DID AS promised, stopping at a store on the way
home so I could grab everything I needed to create. I
wanted to experiment with some of the local flavors to
see how they tasted. Sometimes, I tried something that
was delicious as a batter, but after baking, there was little to
no flavor left at all. Basically, the oven had baked the taste
right out of it. I was curious if that would happen here if I
used fresh ingredients and juices.

"The kitchen is yours, but I hope you know, I'm going
to watch you," Diego said with a grin as he licked a spoon
of vanilla-pineapple cake batter that I'd handed him.

"You can watch. Just know that I get very in my head
sometimes, so if I go quiet, it's just because I'm thinking."

He smiled, licking the spoon clean before dropping it into the sink. "I do the same on the water. Get in my head. Go quiet."

"I wish I could have seen you compete." I waved my hand toward the windows that faced the ocean. "Like, in real time."

I suddenly felt like I'd missed out on this huge part of his life since I was only coming into it now. Surfing had defined him for so long and still did in ways, and I hadn't gotten to witness a moment of it. It made me sad.

"The days were long. And you probably would have been bored. Lots of sitting around, waiting for your turn. And then it's over, just like that." He snapped his fingers.

"I don't think I could ever get bored, watching you surf," I said, still feeling sorry for myself.

"You say that now. But eventually, you'd have been like, *I'm going to go home and bake. See you there.*"

I went to work, mixing and measuring and combining the frosting ingredients with the KitchenAid mixer that I was grateful he had. I knew all of my recipes by heart, so finagling them a bit was easy enough for me to do. I set the mixer on medium and started scooping the vanilla pineapple cake batter into a half-dozen cupcake tray.

"Can I ask you questions while you do that, or will you

mess up?" Diego sat down on one of the barstools that faced me. "And by the way, that batter was delicious."

I smiled. I couldn't help it. "I hope it stays that flavorful. And, yes, I can talk and bake at the same time."

"Do you miss being back home?"

It wasn't at all what I'd expected him to ask. "I've only been gone for a few days, so no."

"What about your sister? You said she runs the bakery with you."

I wasn't sure what Diego was truly getting at or where he was going with these questions.

"I'm sure you miss her."

"You want to know the truth?"

"Always." He leaned forward on his elbows and rested his chin on top of his folded hands.

"I haven't even thought about home since I met you." It was true, and I was only realizing it now, as I was admitting it to him.

He smiled. "Does it make me a dick if I really like hearing that?"

"No," I reassured him.

"Have you told your sister about me?"

"No," I started to say, and his face fell. "But only because I haven't talked to her. I haven't talked to anyone really. They all agreed to leave me alone while I was here. And so far, they've been really good about doing that."

"We should send her a picture though. Don't you think?" He was teasing, but he was also serious.

"Is this because I met your brother? You want to meet my sister?" I asked, putting the cupcake pan into the oven and walking back to the mixer and shutting it off.

The frosting looked perfectly mixed and smelled good. I dipped my finger in the bowl and took a bite. The fresh pineapple juice hit my taste buds, and I smiled before dipping another finger and walking toward Diego, the frosting about to fall off. He leaned forward, took my finger in his mouth, and sucked it clean.

"Holy shit, babe. That is heavenly," he said, and I loved getting that kind of reaction out of him.

"Your pineapples are so flavorful."

"Come here." He wrapped an arm around me and whipped out his cell phone, the camera already open as he held it in front of our faces.

We looked really good together. Like a couple.

He snapped more than one, and then before I knew it, my phone was pinging out text notifications. I grabbed it off the counter and saw his name on my screen. Flipping through the photos, I felt my heart thump even harder in my chest.

"I love these," I admitted, feeling emotional.

"We look hot," he said, and I turned around and agreed. We did. "Now, send one to your family."

"Oh my gosh. You're relentless. All that's going to do is make them ask a million questions," I complained, but I sent one of the pics to my sister anyway.

My phone rang instantly, but it wasn't a call; it was a video chat.

"Look what you did." I turned my phone to face him, and he grabbed it, pressing Accept before smiling into the screen.

"Delilah?" he asked, and she started laughing.

No one called her that, but it was how I had her listed in my phone Contacts. I had no idea why.

"Who are you? Did you kidnap my sister? Turn her into your little island sex slave? And if so, do you have a brother?"

"Diego. Not yet. Yes. Yes, but he's not single."

"Damn, Diego. What good are you?"

"I have a lot of good-looking, single friends if that helps," he said, and I knew he'd won her over with that re-mark.

"Hell yes, that helps! How am I ever supposed to get out

of this town otherwise?"

I ran behind Diego and peeked over his shoulder. "I heard that!"

"Good! God, Spring, it's so boring here without you. And your ex is dating every girl on the planet, and I don't know why, but it's so annoying," she said before making a face. "But I guess it doesn't matter because look at you."

Diego turned to look at me then, giving me a kiss, and Dee gasped.

"You guys look like you've been together forever."

"It kind of feels like it too," he said, and I nodded.

Apparently, we were saying these things out loud, to other people, making them even more real.

"I approve," Dee said, and I was glad she'd called.

The buzzer dinged on the oven, and my eyes widened. "Dee, gotta go."

"Are you baking?" she screamed, and I laughed as I ran toward the oven, grabbing an oven mitt from the countertop.

"Hang up on her, Diego, or you won't get to eat any," I demanded as I pulled them out.

Even without touching one, I knew the cupcakes were ready. I could tell by the smell. I double-checked and gently pressed a finger to the top of one. It sprang back against my touch, and I knew for sure that they were done. "Gotta go,

Delilah. Talk to you later," he said before ending the call.

"Did you just hang up on her?" I asked, a little horrified, and he shrugged.

"You told me to!" he defended himself before adding, "I like her. She's funny."

I was dying to try the cupcakes, so I ripped the top off of one before it even cooled and put it in my mouth. The pineapple flavor was definitely intact but not as strong.

"Here. Tell me if you like this," I said, bringing some of the warm cake to Diego's already-opened mouth.

"Yeah. It's subtle, but you can definitely taste the flavor," he said after swallowing.

"Okay, give me a second."

I walked back toward the warm pan, flipped it over, and separated the cupcakes from each other, so they could cool off. Grabbing a Ziploc bag and a spatula, I spooned some of the frosting into the bag before pressing all of the air out and zipping it closed. I reached for a pair of scissors and cut off one of the bottom corners. The makeshift piping bag always seemed to work in a pinch. I guessed we'd see.

Piping the frosting on top of one of the cupcakes, I watched as it started to melt slightly because I wasn't being patient and waiting. But I was dying to see how they tasted together, and it was killing me to wait for them to properly cool. I took a knife, cut the cupcake in half, put it on a plate, and walked back over toward my man.

He was practically drooling. "If this tastes even half as good as it smells in here, I'm keeping you."

We both grabbed our half and moved it toward our mouths at the same time. Apparently, we were in this together. I took a bite before smiling. The flavors were perfect together, in my opinion.

"Looks like someone can't leave the island," Diego said as he chewed, and I started wondering if I'd even want to when the time came.

SHE CAN'T LEAVE

DIEGO

W E'D GORGED ON Spring's blissful cupcakes before I took her into the pool and fucked her in it. I wanted to have her everywhere. And I never wanted her to leave.

When I woke up this morning and saw her sleeping in my arms, I swore I'd never been happier.

Easing away from her body so that I could go give lessons was brutal but necessary. I planned on showing her some of the local sights and food later, so she'd want to stay here just as much as I wanted her to. I wasn't sure where we were headed, but I knew that I didn't want it to end. I'd already started thinking about when I could fly to California to see her again.

I could do long distance ... I think.

I'd gotten more than a few text messages last night, asking about her, so word had definitely spread around town, if not further. I wasn't shocked, to be honest; I was more shocked that it had taken this long in the first place. My thoughts briefly drifted to Kaylee once more, wondering if she'd reach out or say something and how that would make me feel if she did, but I compartmentalized all that the best I could and put her away.

I wanted to focus on Spring.

When I walked back into the house the morning after my lessons, carrying two coffees, Spring was already awake, up, and sitting outside, watching the ocean.

"You're a goddess," I breathed out against her neck as I placed the coffee in front of her and moved her hair to the side so that I could kiss her.

She spun around, a giant smile on her face. "I hated waking up without you."

She leaped up, wrapped her arms around my neck, and pressed her lips against mine with passion. She kissed me like she'd missed me, and it made me feel so good ... so wanted.

"I loved waking up to you," I teased before pressing a kiss to her nose.

"Thanks for the coffee." She took a sip. "And I had an idea."

"What idea might that be?" I asked before sitting down on a chair and pulling her onto my lap.

"I was thinking that you were right," she said.

I nodded my head. "I like where this is going."

She giggled. "About staying here. There's no way I'm sleeping a single night at the resort when we could be here. So, if your offer is still open …" She paused, and I turned her head to kiss her even though our positioning was awkward.

"Hell yes, it's open. I'll call my brother and handle everything, if that's okay with you," I suggested because he could have her room packed, things delivered, and checked out within the hour.

"That would be nice. Thank you."

"Done," I said before lifting her off my body and placing her back down on the chair. "Don't move. I'll be right back."

I walked inside, reached for my phone, and told my brother everything. He didn't sound shocked, but he still warned me to be careful. Something about falling too hard, too fast, even though that wasn't my MO at all. At least, not usually.

Grabbing a bowl of fruit, I headed back out to where Spring sat, the sound of the waves hitting me instantly. No matter what the ocean did, how angry or vengeful she was, she still brought me comfort. I hated being too far away from her. I respected her. But I didn't trust her. The ocean could turn on you in a heartbeat and with no warning.

"You okay?" Spring asked, and I realized that I was standing still, the bowl of fruit in hand, not moving.

"Yeah, sorry." I started walking again. "I was just looking at the water."

"Me too," she said dreamily.

"Someone from the resort will bring your things to the house," I let her know as I sat down and placed the bowl between us.

"They're going to bring it all here?"

"Yeah."

"That's so nice. Thank your brother for me."

"I was thinking that we could go hiking today. I really want to show you Waimea Falls. And take you to get shaved ice. And shrimp from Kahuku." Her expression shifted, and I smiled. "Too much?" I asked, wondering if I was laying it on thick.

"No. I just like the names of everything. All of that sounds perfect. But I need my luggage because my tennis shoes are in my bag," she said with a grimace.

"No rush, babe. Waterfall isn't going anywhere."

"Will there be a lot of people there?" she asked, and I shrugged.

"Depends. Sometimes, yes, and sometimes, no."

"Okay then." She laughed at my non-answer.

My phone vibrated. I grabbed it, and my heart dropped when I saw Kaylee's name there. She'd sent me a text, and I knew it could only mean one thing—she'd heard. My heart was racing inside my chest, and I suddenly felt awkward in my own skin.

"Diego?" Spring said my name, grounding me.

"It's, uh …" I wondered for a second if I should lie, but I really didn't want to. She'd been nothing but honest with me about her ex, even when it was uncomfortable for her. "Kaylee."

"Your ex?" she said, her voice dropping.

"Yeah."

"Is she calling you? Should I give you space?"

"No, no. It's just a text," I said, still feeling torn in half. "I haven't talked to her in months."

"I know. I remember. Do you think she heard about us and that's why she's reaching out?" Spring asked, and I nodded because that would be the only reason Kaylee had texted. "I'm going to get some water. Do you want anything?"

She was giving me a minute to process, to read the text without her watching me doing it. Spring just kept getting more and more perfect.

"I'm good. Thanks." I gave her a soft smile and watched as she walked away. I wondered what was going through her head.

Pressing on the message button, I swallowed as her text popped up on my screen.

I HEARD YOU'RE DATING SOMEONE, D. I JUST WANTED YOU TO KNOW THAT I'M HAPPY FOR YOU. IT'S ALL I WANT FOR US BOTH.

I wasn't sure what to make of the message. Was it something that required a response? I hadn't been happy at all when I found out she was dating that guy in San Diego, but now? Now, I cared a whole lot less than I ever had before.

Spring walked out slowly, almost unsure if I was ready for her to come back or not, and I jumped up from my chair and handed her my phone. She took it, uneasily at first, but she still didn't look at the screen once it was in her hands.

"Read it, Spring. Read the text."

She moved the phone toward her face, and I watched as her eyes roved across the screen, reading the message more than once.

Handing it back to me, she looked deep into my eyes and asked, "How do you feel?"

"I don't know." It was a cop-out of sorts.

I was feeling all kinds of things, but what if they made Spring feel badly or want to leave? I'd just had her checked out of the resort and said she could stay here, for fuck's sake.

"Do you want to call her?"

"No. Not at all. Honestly," I said, hoping to reassure her. I didn't want to call Kaylee or talk about my personal life with her because it wasn't really her business anymore.

"Can I ask you a hard question?"

"I think so," I managed to say with an uncomfortable laugh.

"If she told you that she wanted you back, that she'd move home, how would you feel?"

It was the most loaded question that could have been asked. One I'd asked myself at least a thousand times before. The answer used to be so simple. I had been so brokenhearted at first that I would have done anything to have her come home. But I didn't feel that way anymore. And that had started before Spring ever entered the picture.

"That used to be the only thing I ever wanted. To hear her say that," I admitted, and Spring nodded, seeming to understand. "But she hurt me too bad to come back from it. I would never trust her again. I'd always be walking on eggshells, waiting for her to tell me that she wanted to leave. We want very different things from life. I couldn't see it then, but now, it's all I see."

I'd never said any of these things out loud to anyone before. I wasn't even sure I'd formulated them in my own mind before this moment. "No matter what, it wouldn't work anymore. What we had is gone. It's broken. And I don't want to fix it."

Spring inhaled long and quietly, blowing it out so slow as she processed my words. "You don't want to fix it? If she wanted to, you'd say no?"

"First of all, she wouldn't want to," I said because it was the truth. Kaylee wasn't the kind of girl to play games or go back to me because her ego was bruised. "But, yeah, I'd say no."

Her hazel eyes started to water, and I closed the distance between us before taking her in my arms and holding her body against mine.

"It's not fair, and it probably sounds really selfish, but I'm so relieved that you'd say no," Spring said, her breath warm against my chest.

I gently pulled her away, so I could see her. "It's not

selfish. It's the same way I feel when you talk about your ex. If you wanted to go home and get back together with him, I think I'd fucking kill someone."

"I shouldn't like hearing that nearly as much as I do," she admitted, and my doorbell rang in the distance.

"Your stuff's here."

THIS IS INTENSE

SPRING

T
HE TEXT MESSAGE and the conversation that had followed was intense. I was scared to death that Diego was going to say I needed to leave, so he could get back together with his ex. It was funny that he'd mentioned the same thing to me, regarding Mitchell. I guessed we were both in the same boat when it came to our previous relationships.

It was early, we'd only just met, but I had feelings for him, logical or not. That much refused to be denied. I heard the wheels of my suitcase being rolled across the tiled floor and Diego yelling that he was bringing it upstairs.

It was official; I was staying here until my flight left.

Jogging up the stairs, I stopped in the bedroom to watch

Diego as he placed my suitcase on top of the bed and unzipped it. He grabbed my makeup bag and brought it into the bathroom before finally seeing me on his way back out.

"How long have you been standing there?"

"Not long," I assured him. "But can I hang my dresses up?"

"You can do whatever you want. That closet is all yours." He pointed toward the closet that wasn't filled with his clothes. I only knew that because I'd seen him grab things out of it before.

I hesitated for a second when I reached the doors before pulling them open. Another woman had lived here. This had been her closet first.

"Don't go there, Spring." Diego's voice pulled me from my thoughts.

"Go where?"

"I know what you're thinking. It used to be hers. But she was barely here. We were barely here. This house was never our home."

I knew I was being unfair and ridiculous, so I tried not to think about it as I opened the door and saw a bunch of empty hangers waiting. There was no trace of her. No garments left behind. Nothing hanging or forgotten about.

"You can take these drawers too." He pointed at the

dresser.

"I feel like I'm moving in," I tried to joke, but it really did feel that way.

"So, do it."

I emptied out my entire suitcase, and Diego moved it into the hallway closet and placed it next to his. It felt like we'd taken a step in acknowledging that whatever this was between us, it wasn't normal. At least, not that I knew of.

"You ready to sightsee or what?"

I looked down, and he was slipping into a pair of shoes.

"Almost," I said before running into the bathroom to braid my hair.

Diego followed. "I sent her a text back. I wanted you to know."

I forced a smile. "Okay. Am I allowed to ask what you said?" Everything seemed so inappropriate, so none of my business, but it didn't stop me from wanting to know.

"I just told her *thank you*. That I was dating someone and I was happy. And I heard she was too."

"That was nice of you," I breathed out, wondering if they would start texting regularly now.

Had he opened a door that would never be closed?

"Did you hear what I said?" he asked as I finished off my second braid, wrapping a ponytail holder around the end.

"Huh?" I looked at his reflection in the mirror.

"I told her I was dating someone."

"Yeah, but I mean, what else were you supposed to say?"

He grabbed my shoulders with both hands and spun me around to face him. "I'm trying to tell you that when you leave to go back to California, I don't want this to end."

"Oh." I stumbled on my words as my heart leaped into my throat, almost making me choke on it. "Oh, so you were serious when you said that you were dating someone. You want to date me?"

"I know you literally just got out of a relationship, but don't you think we should see where this goes?"

I didn't care how asinine this was anymore. Or what people might say or think. My heart was screaming at me to say yes, to give in, to acknowledge that we were more than just an indulgence. Diego felt right. He felt like home. And if that wasn't some kind of sign from God or whoever, I didn't know what was.

"Yes. I don't want this to end when I leave either."

"Thank God, because I had no idea how I was going to let you go."

Something shifted ... *again* ... after admitting that. I

sensed it in the air between us. We'd turned a proverbial corner, growing closer, and wanting more.

"Diego," I said, and he kissed me into silence.

His tongue melted against mine, moving and punishing and making sure I knew who I belonged to, as his hands worked against my skin, each touch more claiming than the last.

He hoisted me onto the bathroom counter, pulled down my panties with one hand, and dropped to his knees. He buried his head between my legs, eating my pussy like his very survival depended on it, as I raked my fingernails against the top of his head, loving the way his hair prickled against me. His five o'clock shadow scraped my inner thighs, and I welcomed the burn as his tongue lapped at me, fucking my hole.

I came fast and hard, convulsing against the cold granite before Diego pulled himself free and pushed inside.

"I can't wait a second longer," he breathed out, and I welcomed him in.

We'd already established that I was on birth control and we were both clean before he had his way with me in the pool the other night, so there would be nothing between us anymore. He fucked me holding me in his arms and the harder he thrust into me, the stronger his grip on me became.

I felt like an extension of his body, moving with him in perfect harmony as he slid in and out, his dick as hard as steel. He grew bigger inside me, and I knew he was about to come. Reaching for the base of his dick, I grabbed it and held it firm.

"Fuck me, Spring. What are you—" he started to say before his words died in his throat, and he came inside me, with force and power, his entire body jerking as I finally released my grip.

"Did you like that?" I whispered against his sweaty neck.

"Fuck yeah, I did." He looked at me and kissed me long and hard.

WE FINALLY MADE it out of the bedroom. I actually would have been content to stay there all day, but Diego had insisted that I needed to see more on the island than just his home. He mentioned shaved ice, shrimp, and waterfalls, and what could be better than that?

So, by the time we finally got to Waimea Falls, it was nice to see it was not particularly crowded. Not that we were alone by any means, but there was enough room for us to swim in the pools and jump off the rocks around the falls.

The funny part about the North Shore was that Diego knew someone everywhere we went. It was like that for me back home in Lake Bliss too. I couldn't go anywhere without running into at least one person I knew. It was the same here but a million times more because Diego was also a famous surfer.

He obliged a few of the fans with photographs at the falls, but then for the most part, people left us alone. The waterfall was romantic. And beautiful. And fun. We swam and held on to one another, and I forgot that we weren't alone until someone whistled, making us laugh.

"I'm a little scared that there are going to be photos posted all over by the time we get back home," he said, and I winced.

"Would it be that bad?" I asked because I wasn't sure what that meant for him.

"No. Just that they will all try to find out who you are and follow you online and stuff."

"All my accounts are private. So, they can find me, but they can't see anything," I said with a smile, and that seemed to calm him significantly.

"They aren't always nice, is all. That was my only worry, babe."

"I get it."

We checked off everything on Diego's list, and he introduced me to everyone he knew along the way. They welcomed me, more than I'd figured they might—since I was a "mainlander" and all. Even the women were kinder than the ones at the resort had been. There were no mean looks, glares, or harsh whispers being spoken behind my back. They genuinely seemed happy for us. Or maybe they were happy to see Diego moving on after having been so brokenhearted. One of them even gave me a puka shell necklace that she'd made by hand, and I swore I was never taking it off.

It felt like Diego and I were an honest-to-God couple, navigating the ins and outs of a brand-new relationship, but I guessed in a sense, that was exactly what we were doing. Being out with him was blissful, the food downright delicious, but I was ready to be back home at his house, sitting in the hot tub, overlooking the ocean as the sun set.

"You ready to go home, babe?" he asked, and I nodded vigorously, loving the way he called his house *home*.

"You read my mind," I said with a smile, and he wrapped his arm around my waist and tucked me up against him, saying good-bye to the last few remaining people around us.

"I like your necklace." He fingered the strand when we reached the truck. "It looks so cute on you."

"I love it," I said, trying to look down at it but failing to see it. I got into the passenger seat, reached for the sun visor, and pulled it down, using the mirror to see the necklace against my throat.

Diego got in, leaned over toward me, and kissed me sweetly. I wondered if I'd ever get tired of being kissed by him. Then, I scolded myself for jumping too far ahead in the future. I hadn't even left the island yet. We hadn't even gotten through a single day of being apart and what it might mean or how we'd feel.

What if our feelings were amplified because we knew there was a time limit on being together? What if none of it was truly real?

"What's going on in that head of yours, Spring?" he asked with a grin as the engine revved to life.

I thought about keeping my doubts to myself but realized that we didn't really do that. Diego and I had been fairly honest and upfront right from the start.

"I was wondering if our feelings were real," I admitted and nodded, making me feel less stupid.

"I wondered the same thing once or twice, if we were just caught up in the moment or something," he said before adding, "but it doesn't feel like a temporary thing to me. Does it for you?"

I admired his profile, taking in the slope of his nose, the scar underneath his eye, his chiseled jawline. "It doesn't."

"How about we make a deal then?" he suggested.

I said, "Okay," before even hearing what it was that I was agreeing to. "Wait. What's the deal?"

"We agree to live in the moment. Enjoy every day we have together until you leave. Then, I'll plan a trip to see you, and we'll see where it all takes us."

"You want to come see me?" I asked through my surprise. "In California?"

"Yes, babe. That's what a long-distance relationship is. We go visit each other. Once you leave here, it will be my turn to come to you. Plus, I know you have a business to run, and it can't be done online, like the majority of mine can."

"You've thought of everything, haven't you?"

"I've just thought of every reason why you might say no and turned it into you saying yes."

I laughed because it was adorable, thoughtful, and downright sexy. This was what men did. They handled their business, recognized their emotions, and went after the things they wanted.

And Diego wanted me. How could I ever say no to that?

TIME TO GO

DIEGO

THE NEXT WEEK had passed us by in what felt like the blink of an eye. I guessed that was what happened when things were so comfortable that they didn't take any extra work.

Spring had made herself at home in my house, and I'd forgotten that I'd ever lived there with anyone else ... or without her. It was like she had always been a part of my life.

We had gone to the local markets, and I let her pick out things to take back home. I refused to let her pay for anything even though she tried. She was my woman, and I wanted to take care of her in every way—that included financially. Lord knew I had enough money to do it—at least three times over—so she'd begrudgingly agreed and then paid me back sexually and with cupcakes. I never complained.

We'd spent the last forty-eight hours basically naked, talking, fucking, and laughing until our cheeks ached. She'd baked for me, and I'd sneakily kept a few of her latest creations to make my brother try them. He was going to flip out when he tasted them. I already had a plan in mind but needed to keep it secret for now.

I stopped Spring mid-pack. "You should leave your things here so you don't have to pack anything when you come back. It will already be waiting for you." I thought it was a great idea, but Spring's face told me otherwise.

She hesitated, thought about it for a second, and simply said, "I'll do that next time."

That was when I knew she wasn't sure that I'd meant everything I said to her. Maybe she thought I'd meant it, but she definitely wasn't convinced that I'd actually follow through. It was fair of her to think that. Even though we'd had an incredible connection and time together, she was well within her rights to wonder what would happen once we were apart.

Me, on the other hand? I had no reservations, no qualms, and no worries. I knew that this was as real as it got.

Distance wasn't going to change anything. It was only going to make me fucking insane, trying to live my life without her.

"I was thinking three weeks. Does that work?" I asked her as I typed on my laptop, searching various airlines.

She bit her bottom lip as she tried to hide her smile but failed. "You mean it?"

"Yes."

"You know I'll have to work though, right? And Lake Bliss isn't that exciting. Are you going to be bored there?" she asked, her tone a little nervous as the thought shifted from being simply an idea to reality.

"I'll hang out in the shop all day. You can teach me how to frost properly," I said, and she laughed because she'd tried to show me how to make their signature swirl, but all I'd done was make a mess all over the counter and my hands.

"I can do that," she said before adding, "Maybe. You might be hopeless in the frosting department."

"Well, I'm a terrific sampler."

"That you are."

"Spring?" I said her name in a serious tone because I hadn't even asked her this or thought about it before now.

"Yeah?" She looked at me with those big hazel eyes, her

hair spilling around her shoulders.

"Is it okay if I come out? I mean, I know your ex will be there. Maybe it's not cool of me to show up there and throw it in his face." I couldn't believe I was even suggesting not seeing her, but the last thing I wanted was to book this trip, look forward to it, and then have her tell me it wasn't a good idea or something before I got on the plane.

She waved me off. "I've thought about that already. I mean, worse comes to worst, we play it low-key, you know? Like, if I hear that he's upset or hurting. But I want you there. I want to see you. I want you to meet Dee, see my shop."

"You're sure?" Now, it was my turn to get a little nervous. To question how in she was for us because I'd already dived in headfirst without a life jacket.

"Yes. I'm positive. Please come out. I'm going to miss you so much," she admitted.

I realized that she was trying to be strong. My girl was trying to hold it all together because what we had between us, it was too much.

"I'm going to miss you too." I pressed *Buy* on my laptop, closed it, and walked over to where she was on the floor, still folding her clothes and placing them neatly inside. "I bought my ticket."

She tilted her head up, and I leaned down and kissed her. Not like it was the last time or I'd never get to do it again because I knew that neither of those things was true. I kissed her like I belonged to her and she belonged to me and that I'd be spending the rest of my life kissing those sweet lips.

"We need to get going. The traffic is sometimes really bad."

Zipping up her suitcase, she reached for my hand, and I helped her up. I watched as she looked around the bedroom, walked onto the balcony, and stepped outside, taking in the view of the ocean and the guys surfing in it.

"I'm going to miss this place," she breathed out, and I wrapped my arms around her, loving the way she fit against me.

"I don't think the house will ever be the same. Not until you come back, that is." I kissed the side of her head and breathed in her scent.

Good-byes really fucking sucked ... even if they were just *see you later*.

Spring laughed when I opened the garage and she saw all the other cars sitting in there. I usually drove my old truck but needed something more reliable and less temperamental to get her to the airport.

"You've been holding out on me," she said, sounding

impressed.

"I forget they're even here until I need them." I realized how douchey that sounded too late. But I hadn't meant it in a dick sort of way. It was true. I rarely drove them. I just liked to look at them.

Now that we were heading to the airport in my blacked-out Audi, I felt like I was dying inside. I held her hand tighter, and whenever I glanced at my passenger seat, she was always staring at me, like I was her favorite thing to look at on the island.

"You're missing the views." I gave a nod out the window, and she grinned.

"No, I'm not."

When we got to the airport, it was a madhouse. I tried to play it cool, like if I could win a surfing world championship at nineteen years old, then I could walk my girl into the airport and put her on a plane without falling apart in the process.

"Diego! Look, it's Diego!"

A few voices filled the air, and I hadn't even remotely prepared for the fact that I might be recognized. Keeping my sunglasses firmly over my eyes, I said aloha and took a few pictures before telling the kids that I needed to get inside.

Spring stood there, watching, a proud smile on her face. "I love how good you are with everyone. They idolize you."

"I always do my best to be gracious. But I don't want to right now," I admitted before grabbing her suitcase from the trunk and taking her hand in mind.

We walked together in silence, the two of us aware of the pain looming once we said good-bye. I started dreading every step, even with the knowledge that I'd see her soon. I didn't want her feeling bad, so I sucked in a long breath and pulled it together, determined to be strong enough for the both of us as we checked in her luggage and stopped outside of the security line.

"Okay. So, this sucks, but I'll see you in three weeks," I said, my voice confident, and she nodded her head before burying it in my chest.

"Three weeks," she mumbled into me.

"Call me as soon as you land," I demanded, my arms wrapping around her.

"I will," she promised.

"I'll miss you, babe."

"I'll miss you too."

I kissed her long and slow, taking my time, my tongue tasting every molecule of her mouth. We pulled apart, dreading it but not saying the words out loud.

I smacked her ass. "See you soon."

I smiled, and she couldn't help but smile back.

"Can't wait," she said before turning away from me.

I stood there, watching her, and she glanced over her shoulder at me before spinning around and running back into my arms.

"I don't want to leave," she said, kissing my neck and holding me tight.

"Then, don't. Stay."

"I love hearing you say that."

"I mean it."

"I know you do." She pulled back, her hazel eyes shining as she leaned on her tiptoes and pressed a kiss against my lips. "Call you when I land."

"Good girl."

And then she walked away. For real this time.

I stood there far longer than necessary. I couldn't see her anymore, but my legs refused to work. My phone buzzed in my pocket. A text from her already, saying how much she missed me and to take care of the house while she was gone.

I was going to fall in love with this woman so damn hard that it was going to kill me if I couldn't have her.

I LEFT MY HEART IN THE NORTH SHORE

SPRING

WAS EXCITED to see Dee waiting for me in her car at the airport. The smile on her face told me that she was dying to hear all about Diego and nothing else.

"I missed you," she said as she helped me with my luggage before hopping in the driver's seat.

The second I'd landed, reality had hit me like a two-by-four to the face. I'd barely thought about work in any sort of boss capacity while I was on the island. But now, being back in my home state, all the responsibility and orders I'd left Dee alone with clouded my mind.

"How's the shop? Was everything okay?" I asked, and she rolled her eyes at me as she pulled out of the busy lot.

"No. It burned down while you were gone," she answered like a smart-ass. "Who cares about the shop? Tell me all about Delicious Diego. That's his name, by the way."

I actually laughed out loud and sent Diego a text, letting him know that I was with Dee for the next thirty minutes and refused to call him while she was around. He responded right away, arguing, and I couldn't stop smiling as I informed him of her new nickname for him.

"Are you texting him? Are you two dating? What is happening?"

"We're seeing where things go," I answered and held my breath as I waited for her reaction. I had no idea if she'd tell me I was crazy or be supportive.

"I hope they go straight back to Hawaii," she said, and I barked out some sort of cough sound.

"What?"

"Nothing." She waved me off with an odd sort of grin. "Bad joke."

"He's coming out here in three weeks," I spat out quickly before I could take it back.

"He is?" Dee practically shouted into the car, smacking the steering wheel with one hand. "This is amazing. You go on your no-longer honeymoon and fall in love while you're there!?"

It sounded so simple when she paraphrased it like that. "Kinda."

"He's really hot. I assume he's nice," she started, and I stared out the passenger window at all the familiar sights.

"Why do you assume he's nice?"

" 'Cause you don't date assholes, Spring," she said very matter-of-factly. "What does he do?"

I cleared my throat. "He used to be a professional surfer."

"He what?" Her jaw dropped open. "Oh my God. I knew he looked familiar."

Turning my head to look at her, my eyes wide, I waited for her to say more.

"You're in love with Diego Peleke?!"

"How do you know who he is?"

"How do you not?" she barked back, and I had no idea how to respond. "Oh, Spring, you're joking, right?" She gave me an incredulous look before blowing out an annoyed breath. "Remember when I went through that Kelly Slater phase?" she asked.

I wanted to slap myself for forgetting that. Dee had become obsessed with Kelly Slater and all things surfing after seeing him on the cover of one of our teen girl magazines in the grocery store. She'd had posters of him all over her walls for years.

"I completely forgot about that."

"Yeah, well, I didn't. And I remember Diego. He's a badass. But I thought he had a fiancée or something."

I shifted in my seat. "He had a girlfriend for a long time. He proposed to her, and she basically said no." I stopped myself from giving Dee too much information on Diego. It didn't feel like my story to tell, and even though she was my sister, I wanted to protect his privacy.

"Damn. Well, her loss is your gain," she said, suddenly even more excited than she'd been before. "How soon can we move? I'm sick of this place."

I had no idea if Dee was joking or if she was serious, but I ignored her question and felt my body growing a little uncomfortable as we neared Lake Bliss.

Had I outgrown it while I was away? Or had we moved on without each other somehow, no longer needing the other to coexist?

"You all right?"

"I feel like I started a new life, and coming back here is like trying to make a circle fit into a square."

"I wondered how it would feel. I mean, you had this

amazing time with this amazing guy, and everything in Bliss is tied up with Mitchell. He's your past, but you've already moved forward." Dee summed it up perfectly.

But what the hell did it all mean?

"What do I do?" I asked, not quite sure even what exactly I was referring to.

Dee shrugged. Clearly, she didn't know either.

THE NEXT MORNING, I opened my eyes and felt the disappointment coursing through me. I was no longer in Oahu. No longer in Diego's bed. And I couldn't hear the ocean outside of my bedroom window. Reaching for my phone, I touched the screen, noticing a text waiting for me.

DIEGO: GOOD MORNING, BEAUTIFUL. I HOPE YOU SLEPT WELL. I MISS YOU.

He was so romantic and thoughtful. I fired off a message back, hoping I wouldn't wake him with it. I hated the time difference between us. The fact that I was three hours ahead of him was brutal.

I got ready for work before Dee was even awake and headed out toward the shop, hoping that I'd feel more at home once I got there.

Plus, I wanted to get an early start on mixing all of the batters and making the week's frostings. It was the first time that baking felt like the actual last thing I wanted to do. Yesterday, I'd been on the balcony, staring at the waves. I had taken pictures of Diego surfing, knowing that once he stepped out of the water, he'd walk straight into my arms. I found myself missing the little life that we'd started to blend together there, and I wondered how long that feeling would last.

The familiarity of the store wasn't enough to pull me from my daydreams. The bakery felt small now, almost suffocating. And it never used to feel that way.

Maybe Dee is right; Bliss is my past, and I've already started stepping forward into my future.

No sooner had the thought entered my mind than I heard a knock on the front door. I peeked around the kitchen wall to see Mitchell standing outside, his hands running through his hair. This wasn't something I'd been prepared for. At all.

I forced a smile as I walked toward the door and unlocked it, letting him in.

"How was it?" he asked first and foremost. "Everything you dreamed it would be?"

Swallowing deep, I said, "And more."

"Hey, look, Spring." He started shifting his weight, clearly uncomfortable. "I just wanted you to hear it from me first."

I was confused. "What? Are your parents okay?"

"Yeah, they're fine. Everyone's fine. I just, um …" He was psyching himself up to tell me whatever he needed to say. "I'm dating Candace."

I almost passed out from relief. For a second there, I'd thought he might insist that we'd made a mistake and want to get back together. Candace had been crushing on Mitchell since she'd first laid eyes on him, and I'd always known it. But she'd never done anything about it as far as I knew.

"I bet she's excited. She's liked you for a long time."

"Is it going to be weird for us now?" he asked.

The first thought in my mind was, *No, because I won't be here,* but I couldn't say that out loud. I wasn't even sure where that answer had even come from or if it was true or not.

"I don't think so, but, Mitchell …" I had no idea how to tell him this part. "While we're being honest with each other …. I met someone on my trip."

"Yeah. Okay, it's weird," he said with an awkward laugh. "I know that's hypocritical of me, but I'm okay with me moving on. I'm not ready to hear that you have."

I actually understood his feelings on the subject. I was the one who had called off the wedding, and we both knew that if I hadn't, we'd be married right now.

"I get it."

"See you around. But kind of hopefully not."

He turned around to leave, and I stood there, watching him go.

Damn. I knew what Mitchell meant, but this town was way too small to avoid each other forever. We could do our best, but at some point, our paths would eventually cross.

Dee walked in the front door right after.

"Was that Mitch?" she asked, looking behind her as she closed the door.

"Yeah. He's dating Candace. He doesn't want to know that I moved on, and he hopes we don't see each other in town."

Dee blew out a loud laugh. "Who knew he had it in him? But I guess we can't stay here forever."

"Why do you keep saying that?"

"Because, Spring, I want to move. I don't want to stay in Lake Bliss until I die. Mom and Dad aren't here. And now that you're not getting married, we don't need to stay."

"What would we do with the bakery?" I asked. *That* was

my first thought, my first reaction, my first question. Quickly followed by, "And where the heck would we go?"

Even though I knew exactly where she was thinking, it seemed like a lot to ask of Diego and to put on his shoulders, no matter how badly he thought he wanted it. What if he eventually didn't?

"I've been thinking about this since you called off the wedding," she admitted, and I had no idea what to say to that.

"You've been thinking about this?" I asked. Apparently, I did have something to say.

"We have two options." She held up two fingers. "One, we sell the bakery, all of our recipes, equipment, name, et cetera. It's a lucrative business, so we'd get six figures for it."

"What's the other option?"

"We close it. Sell everything off piecemeal. Walk away."

"With nothing? Walk away with nothing?" I said, thinking back at how hard we'd worked to build the shop. "There is a third option."

Dee cocked her head to the side. "I'm listening."

"We franchise. Open another store in another location, but we still take earnings from this one."

She nodded. "You're right. That is an option as well."

"Why are we even talking about this?" I exclaimed before throwing up my hands. "I need to finish mixing and baking before we open."

Things went back to normal in Lake Bliss the second I flipped the sign to *Open*. The tourist season was definitely in full effect. The store was packed, and we sold out of multiple flavors well before we were set to close. I made a note to bake more tomorrow so that it wouldn't happen again.

"Was it like this while I was gone?" I asked, horrified at the idea that Dee had been run ragged for ten days without me.

"Honestly, it wasn't. We were busy but not like this," she said, and I felt marginally relieved. "I called in some reinforcements though, so I wasn't alone."

"Oh." I knew I sounded surprised, but it was the first I'd heard of it. "Who?"

"The Merrick twins," she said, and I nodded.

They were high school girls who loved our bakery and had helped us out in the past, usually with on-site events.

By the time we closed the shop, my feet were sore, and my head ached. "I think I forgot what it was like."

Dee laughed. "That quick, huh? Ten days away, and your memory gets wiped clean?"

It sounded idiotic, but it was more than a little true. Ten days and I'd barely thought about the shop or this town unless Diego was asking me about either.

I hopped up onto the counter and put my head in my hands, unsure of where my phone even was. It had been so crazy all day that I hadn't even checked my messages. It was probably in the back, next to the mixing bowls, which needed to be washed.

"I think we should sell the store," Dee said again, unprompted and out of nowhere.

"Again with this?"

"I bet he'd agree with me." She pointed toward the door, a giant smile on her face as I wondered what the heck she was talking about.

"He who?" When I looked up, my heart jumped into my throat. It couldn't be. "Diego?" I breathed out before shoving off the counter and running toward the door.

"What are you doing here?" I asked as I threw myself in his arms, and he lifted me off the ground before placing me on my feet and kissing me senseless.

"I couldn't wait three weeks," he said with a shrug.

GET MY MAINLANDER

DIEGO

WHEN MY FEET finally started working at the airport that day with Spring, they walked me straight to the ticket counter, where I found myself purchasing a flight to California for the next day. I knew I wouldn't be able to wait three weeks to see her, so I figured I had nothing to lose.

I rearranged my schedule, went home to pack a bag, and did my best not to ruin the surprise. I wanted to text Spring and tell her I was coming every five minutes, but I distracted myself instead. My brother came over to my place after I told him I needed to see him, and I practically shoved

Spring's cupcakes down his throat in my excitement for him to try them.

"These are amazing. Local ingredients?" he asked, and I nodded.

"All fresh. All local. All island."

"She has a job if she comes back," he said, and I grinned, but it wasn't quite what I had been going for.

"She's not going to want a job, bruh. She's going to want her own store."

"You sure?" he asked, and I realized that I wasn't.

"No," I admitted.

"Get her back here first, and we'll work out the details. I know you haven't asked, but I've never seen you this happy. Not even with Kaylee," he said, and I put my hand over my heart.

I'd had no idea how much I needed to hear that.

"Thank you. I've never felt like this before, but you can never be too sure. I appreciate hearing it."

"Go get your mainlander and bring her home." He slapped my back, and I sucked in a breath.

That was exactly what I was going to go do.

I FOUND THE store and Lake Bliss easily—with Delilah's help. She'd reached out to me online, insisting that we be friends, while Spring was on her flight back, which worked out perfectly because I'd needed to tell someone that I was on my way out there.

"I can't believe you're here," Spring said.

Even though it had barely been a day, I'd missed her smile and infectious energy. There was something about being near her that settled all the scattered pieces in me.

"I can't be away from you," I said before tilting her chin up again and kissing her.

She smiled up at me, her cheeks turning red from my words.

"It's a really cute town. *Busy.*" I emphasized the last word.

"Tourist season," she said, and it finally made sense, what she had said about our hometowns being similar.

"Excuse me. Introductions. Hellooooo?" Dee said.

I walked away from Spring and over to her, pulling her into a bear hug. She and Spring definitely resembled each other.

"Sister."

"Brother," she said back, and Spring's head ping-ponged between the two of us in confusion.

"Have you guys been talking?" She jutted out her hip and narrowed her eyes.

"A little," Dee admitted before asking, "Do you know Kelly Slater?"

Spring walked over and swatted her arm to get her to be quiet.

"Don't listen to her," she directed before hopping onto the counter.

I laughed. "I do. He actually lives next door when he's in town."

"He what?" Spring shouted, and I wondered if we were going to have to move. I couldn't have my biggest competition for her affections living in the house next to ours. "You never told me that."

"You never asked." I shrugged. "Do you have a crush on Slater? I can't deal with that, if I'm being honest."

Dee giggled. "She does not. I do. I have the crush. Me."

"Thank God. The guy still competes, and I'd hate to have to hurt him."

"Oh, I like you so much," Dee complimented, and I felt my chest swell.

I gave Dee a wink. "I like you too."

If I'd thought meeting Spring was *too* much, *too* comfortable, *too* perfect, Dee only added to it.

I looked around their store, taking in all that they had built together, and felt the same kind of pride that I only assumed Spring felt whenever she saw my surfing trophies and photos.

"This place is amazing." I walked around the small space, taking note of the way everything was color-coordinated and perfectly designed.

Dee waved a hand. "Yeah, but we're bored of it. Thinking about selling," she said, and Spring's mouth dropped open before she slammed it shut.

I stared at Spring, her hazel eyes avoiding mine. "Is that true? You're thinking about selling the bakery?"

She finally looked at me but quickly looked away. "I don't know. Dee won't stop talking about it, and I literally just got back here."

"I was merely suggesting that maybe it was time for us to leave Bliss," Dee said with a sly grin.

I swore my heart jumped out of my chest and started flopping around on the floor, like a fish out of water, hoping to be saved.

"Why?" I took a step toward where Spring sat. "Why would you leave Bliss?" I pushed, wanting to hear everything that could have possibly developed in the last twenty-four hours, but Spring stayed quiet.

Dee exhaled loudly, drawing my focus toward her. "She isn't marrying Mitchell anymore. Our parents moved out of Bliss years ago. I'm never going to meet anyone and have an actual boyfriend if I stay here. Spring's new boyfriend lives in another state. It's time for us to go."

I found myself laughing a little. "Why can't you have a boyfriend here? What's wrong with you?"

"Hey!" she shouted. "Nothing is wrong with me. I'm not attracted to any of the guys here. We've all known each other forever. And all the new men who do move into town are already married and want to raise their dumb kids here. I'll be perpetually single if we stay, baking cupcakes for weddings that I'm never going to have." She groaned and made her voice do that frog-like sound.

"You're so dramatic," Spring finally said.

I tossed her a look. "What are your thoughts on all of this?"

"I've had, like, two seconds to think about it," she answered, and I hated her response.

But maybe she thought she was pushing herself on me and that I didn't want her to come back to Oahu with me.

"Well, I have some information that might help sway your decision."

Dee's eyes grew wide as she slapped her hands together.

"Tell us! Tell us! Kelly Slater wants me to have all his babies, and we must start right away 'cause he's getting old?"

Smiling, I looked at my girl again. "We might have to keep her locked up in the garage."

"Clearly," she said with a grin.

"Diego!" Dee snapped. "Tell us."

I nodded. "Once I got back home, I called Samson," I said before looking at Dee. "That's my brother. He owns the resort Spring was staying at."

"Oh. Okay," Dee said.

"I had him try some of your cupcakes, and he said that you have a job if you want it with the resort. Or I'm sure that we could find a space to open a store. Or I was even thinking that a cupcake truck might be really cool."

"Like the shrimp truck we ate at?" Spring sounded more than a little excited.

"Exactly."

Dee walked over toward her sister, pushing me out of the way a little before grabbing her hands. "Seriously. Why would we stay when our lives aren't here anymore? We can sell the shop. And we can either sell the rest of the property and land or keep it so that it stays in the family. We can rent it out."

"I don't mean to interrupt, but how lucrative is the

bakery?" I asked, putting on my business hat. "And I only ask because if you can sell it and make good money, then I don't think you should sell the land. Real estate is always a smart investment. Especially in a place like this that is clearly still growing."

They both stared at me, taking in my words, and I felt the need to say one last thing. "I'm also not trying to tell you girls what to do. And if you were saying that you wanted to move to the North Shore, you don't need money because you wouldn't have to pay for anything there. But I'm getting ahead of myself because neither one of you said you wanted to leave here and go there in the first place."

I started feeling nervous. The same way I had before catching my first wave in a competition.

Spring hopped down from the counter and put her hand on my cheek. "Not a chance I move away from here and not go straight to wherever you are. But do you want me there?"

"Us." Dee cleared her throat. "Do you want *us* there? This is a package deal, buddy."

"Yes. I want you there. Both of you," I said before whispering in Spring's ear, "But mostly you. Please come home."

Spring's eyes were filled with moisture as she faced her sister. "Let's do it. Why not? You only live once, right?"

EPILOGUE

SPRING

THE NORTH SHORE
SIX MONTHS LATER

TODAY WAS THE big day. Dee was finally arriving on the island and moving into the house with Diego and me. It was big enough that we'd all have our space, and I liked the idea of her staying with us … at least for now.

She had basically forced the two of us out of the bakery that night, insisting that I start packing. She told me that it was my job to set up our new digs in Oahu while she handled closing everything for us in Bliss.

It wasn't that easy, obviously. Diego went back to the

island without me while Dee and I worked out exactly what we were going to do with our family land and the cupcake store. We decided to keep the property, like Diego had suggested.

Lake Bliss was so infinitely popular with no signs of slowing down that we knew using it as a vacation rental would be lucrative. It made things easier on us anyway—to keep the house furnished and not have to deal with that side of things. It wasn't like we needed anything more than our clothes and shoes to move anyway. We weren't moving into an empty apartment.

Dee and I also decided to sell the bakery, most of my recipes—some things needed to be sacred—equipment, and the name outright in one deal. We wouldn't be silent partners, have ownership claims, or anything at all. It would be like we were never there in the first place.

It felt like the best option in terms of truly moving forward. For everyone. Even though Mitchell would never admit it, I knew that he was relieved that we wouldn't be running into one another for the rest of our lives. Mitchell was never leaving Lake Bliss, especially once he took over his father's company.

I was grateful that Dee had offered to handle selling the business and to stay back for a few months until the new owners got on their feet and learned the ropes. She wasn't willing to walk away and not look back. We had built a successful business, and Dee wanted it to stay that way.

The Merrick twins heard about us leaving, cried, and then convinced their parents to buy the bakery. Luckily for them, their parents were loaded and basically retired. They had opened up one of the original hotels before selling it to a big corporation for a lot of money. The four of them planned on working at the bakery until the girls were old enough to take it over. They'd paid us close to a million dollars, which, to be honest, was a bit of a steal, considering the bakery cleared over half a million each year and had the potential to do much more.

"Are you nervous?" Diego walked into the kitchen, where I was trying out a new flavor I couldn't get quite right, and wrapped his arms around me. "She'll be here soon."

"I know." I turned around and dropped some frosting on his nose before licking it off.

"Don't start something you can't finish, babe."

"Think she'll be pissed we didn't pick her up?" I asked, suddenly concerned that we had been rude by not going to the airport to greet her.

"Uh, did you see who I sent to get her?" he asked, and I

started laughing.

No, it wasn't Kelly Slater. Thankfully, he wasn't in town. But it was another surf pro, who was single and far too willing to pick her up and pretend to be a driver. Did I mention how hot he was? Yeah, Dee wasn't going to be mad at all.

When the front door flew open and I heard Dee's voice echo in the air, I stopped my baking failure and ran to greet her.

"You're here!"

She stopped walking and stared at the space that I'd grown used to. "I can't believe this is where we live," she said before hugging me. "And thanks for the driver. Holy shit, Spring, you sent Kai to pick me up?"

"Yeah, I know." I glanced over her shoulder to see him walking in with some of her bags. "Are there more?" I asked, already knowing the answer.

"I literally brought everything I owned that wasn't staying at the rental. So, yeah, there's more."

"Sister." Diego appeared, a giant grin on his gorgeous face.

"Your house is fucking brilliant. No wonder Spring didn't want to leave."

"Thanks. I love it," he said before pulling me tight

against him the way he always did.

"What's with the cupcake truck outside, bruh?" Kai asked as he carried in more of Dee's bags.

"That's ours. We're bakers," I said.

Kai started wiping at the corners of his mouth, his long, sun-bleached hair falling into his eyes.

"You bake?" he asked, looking straight at Dee and not me.

"You surf?" she fired back, and he laughed.

After sitting down with Diego and talking all of our bakery options out, I'd realized that I didn't want to be here, in the North Shore, with him, stuck in a shop six days a week from sun up to sun down. The idea of having an actual storefront felt exhausting. What if we wanted a day off?

And while I appreciated Samson's offer to bake for the resort, I hadn't worked for someone else since I was a teenager. I didn't think I could do it anymore. I'd been my own boss for too long.

Thankfully, I called Dee, and she agreed, having all the same concerns I did. Our new life required changing the way we worked and how we wanted to spend our days. And honestly, it wasn't like we needed the money. We were choosing to do this because we enjoyed it and because not working felt more than a little lazy.

So, I'd bought a food truck, had it converted on the inside to what was required for baking and mixing, gotten all of the business licenses we needed for cooking and selling, and finally gotten it painted. The Island Cupcake Truck was born. We were equipped to handle corporate events, weddings, birthday parties, and if we wanted, parking on location for a day and having customers come to us. Dee was going to start building our social media following within the next week.

The best part was, we were in control of how much and how often we wanted to work. I had no idea how it would all pan out, but I wasn't worried about it. Life seemed to have a way of coming together in ways you least expected.

"Hope you're not tired, sis, 'cause we're having a bit of a party tonight," Diego said from his position over my head.

"We are?" I pulled out of his grip and gave him a surprised look.

"Welcome to the North Shore, Monroe sisters."

"I hope he's coming." She thumbed toward Kai, and Diego just laughed.

"Are you kidding? I'll be first in line," Kai said, looking right at my sister with that familiar gleam in his eyes.

Oh shit.

Here we go.

THE END ✾

Thank You

Thank you so much for reading my story for spring. I think it might be one of my favorites! Who doesn't want to go to the North Shore and fall for a super hot surfer?! LOL I hope you enjoyed reading Diego & Spring's love story. I came up with the idea for my Fun for the Holiday's Collection to give you lighthearted, happy reads that you could get lost in. I know that the world has been crazy lately, hopefully this helped you escape… if only for a little while. <3

About the Author

Jenn Sterling is a Southern California native who loves writing stories from the heart. Every story she tells has pieces of her truth in it as well as her life experience. She has her bachelor's degree in radio/TV/film and has worked in the entertainment industry the majority of her life.

Jenn loves hearing from her readers and can be found online

at:

Blog & Website:

www.j-sterling.com

Twitter:

www.twitter.com/AuthorJSterling

Facebook:

www.facebook.com/AuthorJSterling

Instagram:

@AuthorJSterling